Words From My Mind

front three
ever old went morning
small looked
room looked going
must good real coming
Boy seemed called door never huge see
make something also take enough
wonder Mr remember bad
big thought day asked course
time right people first just almost
Tom life get know money much
house well last Hey
week made job go really
guys Dad told next two
place wanted felt back tell saw
took every guy better
heard years ten days hope Sarje
want probably think hours
now Army floor another God
Sophie one like thing
wife look white
new Barney Pittsburgh decided local
found around way car
someone lot Mom got letter Oh
food usually many man
name came church beer times
pretty night home guess four
Charlie eat may sure
couple Well little Father
today knew always Maybe put
long anything
believe getting figured
least call Aunt still looking
even
tried received

by
Ed Folino

Dedication

I'd like to dedicate this book to the people out there who want to write a book or have written a book and would like to get it published. Have faith in God and yourself and never give up. It could happen for you.

Ed Folino
2015

The Contents

Humor

BASIC TRAINING - 1963

Beer

In 1962, my friends and I were sitting at our local ballfield drinking Iron City beer. Iron City was the local brewery in Pittsburgh, Pennsylvania, my hometown.

We were seventeen, but always managed to find someone older to buy us beer. What we didn't finish drinking we'd sell to other guys at a premium price. The money we made on these sales was used to purchase more beer, or an occasional bag of greasy Snyder's potato chips. My two friends and I did everything together, including selling our blood, to buy more beer.

My friend Mike had a nickname of "Fingers." He had very, very long fingers and he used them sometimes for retail theft to get money to buy – what else, more beer. Ray was a sort of quiet guy who was always philosophizing about things he knew nothing about. Me, I was just there to drink beer. I was somewhat normal, I would say. Anyway, none of us had jobs and we would just bum money from our friends who did to buy beer.

This particular night, Ray had a brainstorm. He suggested, "Why don't the three of us join the Army?" He added, "We could do our civil duty, and make money to buy more beer." He said his brother went in the Army on the "buddy plan." If the three of us signed up together, the Army would guarantee that we would be stationed together for the first year of our two year enlistment.

The normal enlistment was three years. If

we agreed to move our names to the top of the draft list our enlistment would only be two years. Basically, we were telling the U.S. Army to draft us. What a plan! This may have been the best thing I ever did. At the time the Army was taking volunteers for Vietnam. By the time my two year enlistment was over they were taking every available body for a thirteen month tour of Vietnam.

I always wondered why they called it a tour. I guess you were, in reality, touring these people's country. Although I don't think there are too many tours where you shoot at men and they shoot back at you. Anyway, we signed up at our local City-County building and waited for our draft papers from Uncle Sam.

The Physicals

We continued to work on our beer drinking while anxiously awaiting our draft notices. All three of us received our papers on December 10th. Our day of induction was January 9th, 1963. But first we had to have a thorough physical exam to see if we qualified as able-bodied volunteers. The physicals were scheduled for December 15th.

Prior to our physicals we practiced our beer drinking vigorously. In fact, we drank until 6 in the morning. We were scheduled to get our physicals at 8, just two hours later. Needless to say we were probably legally drunk when we showed up.

My sly buddy Mike managed to sneak a six-pack of Iron City into the City-County building. He put it in a stall in the men's room on the first floor. He locked the door and crawled under it.

What a genius! In 1963, security was a lot different than it is today.

I am a little modest, but I was shocked when I was told to strip to my underwear. Hey, what the hell, I was stoned, so I guess it didn't bother me that much.

All the guys there were issued a number. We had to report to different floors and doctors. There were about 150 of us present that day. We were broken down in groups of ten. Neither Mike nor Ray was in my group. Besides the physical testing they had a written exam. I guess the Army wanted to see if we were smart enough to be shot at.

We had a half hour break around noon and I met Mike and Ray at the cafeteria. I got a little surprise when I talked to them. It seems Mike failed the written exam. He said he kept falling asleep and he didn't answer all the questions. This might have been true, but I doubt it. Mike was expelled from St. Kate's school in the seventh grade. He missed half of the school year playing hooky. Well, there goes one from the buddy plan. I guess it was just Ray and I.

I could see Ray's mind working. I was shocked when he decided to join the Air Force instead of the Army. "Ray, are you nuts? The Air force is a four year enlistment," I said. But his mind was made up. I think he was the most intelligent of all of us. Ray said if he went to the Air Force they would pay for a college education.

So there I am, one part of a three-part buddy enlistment plan. I didn't know what to do. I had already passed the written exam, so I couldn't fail it at that point. I had to come up with a plan. I didn't want to go in the Army by myself.

The Plan

I went to the men's room where the beer was waiting for me. I drank four of the six beers there. I had three more stations to visit before I was accepted for military duty. I was sailing pretty well after the four beers. I figured if I acted goofy enough at these stations they would maybe ask me to go home. Fat chance!

At the end of the third station everyone but I was told they were done with their testing. I was told to report to room 205. I figured my plan had worked, and they were going to tell me to go home. There were four chairs in room 205. Two seats were occupied. About every ten seconds this one guy would yell out a cuss word. I figured he may have been drunk also. The other guy just kept staring at me. He would alternate between a mean stare and a goofy looking frown. I thought to myself, "Where the hell am I?"

When I entered the door it had the room number and the doctor's name. I looked up at the inner office door which read, "Dr. Saul Rueben, Doctor of Psychiatry." I thought to myself, "They think I'm crazy!" I knew I wasn't crazy, but they weren't sure. I had a brainstorm. If I acted crazy, I was sure to fail my physical. I knew those other two guys were probably nuts, so why not me.

I was the first to be called even though I was the last to enter. Dr. Rueben weighed about 400 pounds. He came out of his office and asked me to go in. He sat in a very small chair where the cheeks of his rear end flopped over to each side. Once he sat down, he never looked me in the face again. He smoked about seven cigarettes while I was in there. He just kept asking questions while puffing away, and letting the ashes fall on his shirt cuff. At one point I asked him if I could smoke. He snarled back, "You can't smoke in a government office!" I thought it was good to be getting on his bad side.

He was really interested in my dreams. I thought to myself, "Now here's my chance to act like a loon." I told him I always dreamed that I was Superman or Batman. I told him I dreamt about water quite a bit. I told him I always dreamt I was on an elevator and the cables snapped. He told me if I ever hit the bottom of the shaft I would probably die of a heart attack. I said, "I guess I never did, 'cause I'm still here." He was not amused.

He asked about my home life. I told him I hated my mother, which wasn't true. I told him I hated her because she wouldn't let me use her car or buy me beer.

I saw a form on the desk which read, "Application for military duty." He raised his chubby hands and stamped it "Approved." I thought, "What kind of guys are they letting in the Army today?" Well, so much for that plan. I guess I'm going into the U.S. Army by myself.

Induction and the Train

I got my affairs together and reported to the Pennsylvania Train Station. My mother and step-father were with me. I remember her crying. I should have been the one who was crying. I really didn't want to go. I had screwed up royally.

This huge General told us to say our good-byes. I later found out he was a Master Sergeant. He looked like a General to me though. What did I know?

All the inductees, including myself, were put in a small room to be sworn in. It was scary. Two years of my life would be wasted.

In the Army they have something called, "Police Call." It means that you walk around with your eyes to the ground and pick up trash and cigarette butts from the ground. I was only in the Army for thirty seconds, and I'm doing Police Call already. It was my first Police Call of the two to three thousand I did in two years.

All the new army privates boarded the train to Augusta, Georgia to report for Basic Training. I was very popular on this train ride. I knew it would be hard to smuggle a case of beer on the train. My step-father bought me a fifth of Canadian Club as a send-off. I guess he was glad to see me go since I was always drinking his beer. Anyway, I put the fifth in my suitcase and sold shots for a dollar a piece. Things were looking up a little.

Reporting for Basic Training

The first thing we did after getting off the train was what else: Police Call. I guess they thought we didn't do it well enough at the Pittsburgh train station. After I was in the Army for awhile I figured why we had so many Police Calls. If our superiors didn't have anything for us to do it was a fantastic time consumer.

We took a bus from the train station to Fort Gordon, Georgia. This would be my home for the next eight weeks. The bus dropped us off at a huge auditorium and thirty or forty other buses already there. We were told to sit anywhere. Of course the only empty seats were in the first few rows.

There were five men on the stage attired in dressy uniforms. I figured this one guy must have been a General because the other four were sucking up to him. It turned out he was a Captain. If anything, I hoped they would teach me how to tell what rank these guys are.

Well the Captain said he was going to call out names. He said, "If you hear your name called, say 'here.' I don't want to hear, 'over here,' 'that's me,' 'present,' or anything else, only 'here.'"

I found out it was an Army custom to say your last name first, and your first name last. The Captain then called the first name, Charles, James. The guy says, "Yo." Everyone in the hall laughed; big mistake. We got a fifteen minute lecture on following orders and respect for a superior officer.

My last name is relatively easy to pronounce, "Fo-li-no." Actually it's pronounced like "Fo-lee-no." Anyway, after mutilating a bunch of other names he says, "Fleeno, Flineno, Foieeno, Edward." I said, "Here." He never did ask me how to pronounce it. We were then each issued a number and told to report back to our buses. This was our service number. It identified me then and when I applied for Social Security benefits over a year ago. I still remember it to this day, US52566484.

I then realized that I was getting a little hungry. More importantly, I was getting thirsty for a beer. I didn't know it at the time, but I would not drink another beer for almost three weeks. If I would have known that then I would have resigned right on the spot.

A Little Hair Trim and New Duds

We took a five minute ride to another building. It was called, "Initial Processing." It was a fancy name for a shoe store, barber shop, and clothing store.

First we received a haircut. Even the guys with crew cuts got a haircut. I struck up relations with a few of the guys on our frequent bus rides. After they received their haircuts I hardly recognized them.

One guy looked like an 8-ball. Another looked a great deal like Yul Brenner. I had a huge widow's peak. After I got buzzed I looked like Igor from the many horror movies I had seen. I had a nice head of hair and it broke my heart.

Some guys were actually crying. I thought, "It's not the end of the world." The army was actually before their time. Now, a lot of men think very short hair or shaved heads are cool.

We were then escorted to the largest quantity of green clothing you could imagine. In the Army everything was green. They had a typical sophisticated army name, "Olive Drab." Boy, they weren't kidding. It was the drabbest color I've ever seen. I figured the green color was so any enemy couldn't see you in the jungle. I didn't know about any one else in that room, but I didn't plan on running around in any jungle.

First we were sized for boots. Then we proceeded to the clothing line. We were handed a duffle bag. This was an olive drab, what else, canvas bag to stuff all my new duds in.

There was a little guy behind the first table who must have been reincarnated as a master tailor. He took one look at me and said, "Extra large." I listened as he looked at the guy behind me and he repeated, "Extra large." The guy must have weighed about fifty pounds less than me. It really didn't matter. All the clothes were Extra-super-large. I flopped around in these clothes for eight weeks. I didn't know it at the time, but I was making a fashion statement wearing floppy clothes like the kids do today. Well, it was another momentous adventure. I can't wait to see what comes next.

My New Home, D-4-2

Here we go, more numbers and even a letter this time. The D stands for our battalion, the 4 was our company, and the 2 was our platoon. I don't know if this is exactly right. It has been forty-six years; I do know it was D-4-2. I had to scream it often enough that I couldn't forget that.

The barracks looked a lot different than the promotional photos I'd seen. It did have the shiniest brown floor I've seen. It was like a mirror. I thought they had a maintenance crew come in to wax and buff it. Silly me. I didn't know we had to shine our own floors. It turns out there were a great deal of things I didn't know. I also didn't know that you never volunteer for anything.

At our first formation our platoon Sergeant asked if anyone knew how to paint. I raised my hand. This was a huge mistake. I was told to report to the mess hall immediately. For four days I and four other morons were to paint the mess hall. We started painting at 0600 hours every morning until 2200 every night for four days. So while everyone in my platoon was learning to march I was painting.

If you're wondering what 0600 hours and 2200 hours means, that is 6 in the morning, and 10 at night. That's military time. They gave us a chart to tell us how to read and interpret military time. Why should the Army tell time like the rest of the world? They had a twenty-four hour clock. No AMs or PMs for them. We were also given a chart with the ranks of all enlisted men and officers. It also showed the proper way to salute an officer. Saluting an officer was very important. This chart did not tell me when not to salute an officer.

I was up on a ladder painting the roof overhang on the Mess Hall. I saw an officer approaching. I think he was Major. I was petrified and shaking uncontrollably. Maybe he wouldn't look up at me and I wouldn't have to salute him. He looked up at me. I immediately saluted him, but forgot I had the paint brush in my hand. I slapped white paint all over the side of my face. He tried very hard not to laugh. He just smiled at me and returned my salute. What the chart did not tell me is that when on a work detail you don't have to salute an officer. Nice going fellas'. I swore that I wouldn't volunteer for anything again.

The Sarge

Sergeant Biggs was a small man with a very red face. His hands shook constantly. I found out that he was a career Army man, and a career boozer. He loved to drink beer. Ah, I had found a new idol.

After I got to know him better he offered me one very important cure for a hangover. He took a woman's Midol pill every morning. He said it took care of his bloated feeling and cramps. It's a shame he didn't have a pill for his shaking hands.

The Corporal

Corporal Heinz was an evil person. He enjoyed seeing people in pain. He had a very strong southern accent. I don't know why. I found out later that he was born and raised in Washington, DC. I guess he lived on the south side of town. He was very hated by all of the guys in our platoon. I lot of them would have liked to punch him, but they knew it was an instant trip to the Army stockade (jail).

After basic training a lot of the guys returned to Fort Gordon for Signal School training. A few of the guys who returned found out that Corporal Heinz was not actually a Corporal. He was an acting Corporal. He was a Private, the same as us, but assigned to our platoon as a Corporal. These same guys spotted him in a Post beer parlor and followed him out one night. They didn't kill him, but they beat him up pretty bad. We were told they told him his beating was compliments of D-4-2. I think he got the message.

I Am Not Alone

Well, it turns out I had a few guys in my platoon from my part of Pittsburgh. There was Junior P. from Beechview, and Vic J. and Danny D. from Brookline. Beechview was where I came from and Brookline was only a few miles away.

Junior, Vic, and I volunteered for the draft, but Danny was actually drafted. Junior, Vic, and I were all seventeen years old and Danny was twenty-four. I didn't loaf with any of these guys at home, but we all knew some of the same guys. It was nice to have someone to talk to about home.

A Few More Comrades

There were all kinds of personalities, races, and ethnic backgrounds in the army. We had two guys from Tennessee. Joe J. was from Memphis and Bill C. was from Chattanooga. Joe J. was a real character. He looked and acted like Wally Cox (Mr. Peepers). Bill C. had an oval face with thick glasses and a million freckles. He was always smiling or laughing. I don't know how he was accepted for military service with his bad eyes.

Jimmy M. was from Ft. Walton Beach, Florida. He was the ladies man. Monroe B. was from some little city in Alabama and was one miserable individual. We had two homosexual guys in the mix also. I don't recall their names. They were both over six feet tall and one guy was black and the other guy was white. I do remember their names starting with the same letter. I'll call them Dick and Darryl. They liked each other very much and did everything together.

There was Gary G. from Dallas, Texas; no one could pronounce his last name. I can't forget Ulysses G., my bunkmate. I slept on the top bunk and he slept on the bottom. He was a really nice guy. Then we have Charlie C. from Tulsa, Oklahoma. Charlie had the strongest southern accent I've ever heard and he laughed constantly. You couldn't help liking Charlie.

There will be more on all of these guys later on. I don't want to get too ahead of myself.

The Mess Hall

Leave it up to the Army to call food "Mess." Some of the things they served us did look like a mess. Every company had their own mess hall. Our mess hall was the nicest looking one on the Post. That's because some idiots volunteered to paint it. We had roughly 300 men in our company and all of us had to get in line, get our food, eat it, and be out of in ten minutes.

Corporal Heinz was in charge of, you might say, moving us along. If we got five minutes to eat, that was a stretch. The Corporal would walk around each table observing us eating. If he thought you weren't eating fast enough he always said the same thing. He would say, "Are you done eating yet?" Our usual reply was, "No." He would say, "Yes you are, now get the hell out of here." Many times I would be walking out finishing the food on my tray. Boy, I really hated that guy.

For breakfast they usually had assorted dry cereals. Some mornings we would have oatmeal. We would usually have eggs, bacon, sausage, and some king of strange potatoes. I do remember that the sausages were excellent.

I don't think any of the cooks knew how to make fried eggs. They were always scrambled. I remember this hoity-toity guy said, "I would like a couple poached, please." The whole cooking staff was rolling on the floor in hysterical laughter.

They always posted a menu in the front of the entrance to the mess hall. This one particular morning I saw a strange item listed on the menu, "Creamed Chipped Beef on toast." It turns out it was chipped beef in a creamed sauce over toast, or a biscuit. I loved it, except when the cook substituted water instead of milk for the cream sauce. Sometimes they even subbed ground meat instead of beef. There must have been a chipped beef shortage that day.

Lunch was the big meal. They called lunch "dinner." Dinner was called "supper," and was usually a cold plate with soup. The soup was always good. It contained all the leftovers from a week's past menus.

You could eat in any mess hall on the Base that you wanted to. I don't know why anyone would. I found out that the same menu was served every day in every Army Base in the entire United States. The Army had a group of dieticians who put together every meal. They were supposed to be perfectly balanced.

I'm of Italian descent. The Italians have a dish called, "Pasta Figoli." It can be any kind of pasta made with tomato sauce mixed with garbanzo beans. I think one of these dieticians must have been an Italian wannabe. Every time we had any kind of pasta on the menu there were always green peas as a side vegetable. Some hose bag thought he was making Pasta Figoli.

I remember one lunch (a.k.a. dinner) when they put a huge pile of steak on my plate. I was shocked. They never served that much of the main course, especially steak. I took it to my table and got ready to dig in. I bit into my steak, and immediately spit it out. Charlie C. was sitting beside me. "What's the matter with your liver, Hoss?" Charlie called a lot of guys Hoss. I guess it was an Oklahoma slang word. I said, "Liver! That's why they gave me so much of it." Charlie said, "I love liver." I traded him my liver for his mashed potatoes and baked beans. Problem solved.

There were many jobs to be done in the mess hall. Every week there was a schedule on our bulletin board designating when and who was scheduled for KP. KP was yet another great Army name. KP stood for Kitchen Police. No one in the company was exempt from KP duty. If you were assigned KP duty you had to use a white towel and tie it to your bunk. When the Mess Sergeants would go through the barracks in the morning he could find your bunk. If you were on KP you were awakened a couple hours before everyone else, and it was always dark at that hour.

The Mess Sergeant always carried a small flashlight to find who had a towel tied to the end of their bunk. A few times, if I came in late, I would put a towel on someone else's bunk. It never worked. Besides, the guy's bunk where I tied the towel to would get pretty mad when they tried to wake him up at 4 in the morning.

There were three basic jobs for KP duty: "DRO," which meant "dining room orderly," "cooks helper," and finally "pots and pans man."

DRO was the easiest job. DROs were in charge of keeping the dining room clean. Those who arrived at the mess hall first in the morning usually got the DRO job. I never got a DRO job. Cooks helper wasn't that bad though. It depended what Mess Sergeant you were working for.

The worst job was the pots and pans man. The guys who reported last were always assigned to pots and pans. I was always assigned to pots and pans. I really did well at it after a while. I had plenty of experience. The most important job of the pots and pans man was the removal of all the grease from the pots and pans. Most Mess Sergeants would wear a pair of white gloves to rub over the pots and pans. If they saw grease on the gloves they would usually say "Do 'em again." The biggest secret to getting excess grease off pots and pans was the use of lemons. I would put a bunch of lemons in my rinse water, and they would absorb all of the excess grease from the pots and pans. I know you women who may be reading this know this already. But for you men, if you're ever assigned KP by your wives, you can dazzle them with this little kitchen helper.

The Army cooks used an exuberant amount of grease when cooking. I think they may have still been using lard back in 1963. Well, all this grease went to the "Grease Pit." It was located outside the kitchen, and it had to be cleaned out daily.

The platoon Sergeants used cleaning the grease pit as a punishment for guys that had earned it. But if there weren't enough screw-ups available, one of us was assigned this chore. If you drew the grease pit duty you were issued a pair of heavy duty gloves and flood boots that went up to your crotch. You had to crawl down inside this pit and take all the grease out, and put it in a drum. It was a really nasty, smelly, crappy job.

No one knows what ever happened to the used grease. I think they sent it to this restaurant in Augusta which sold ten hamburgers for a dollar. You couldn't wear a long sleeve shirt when you ate one of these burgers. When you bit into one of those suckers, the grease would roll down your arm. You needed at least twenty napkins when you sat down to eat there. Twenty napkins were usually enough when you ate ten burgers. That's two per burger. As bad and unhealthy as these burgers were, they packed the restaurant every night. Hey, I was good for at least twenty of them.

Inspections

We had weekly barracks inspections and were graded on the cleanliness and neatness of our barracks. Our bunks had to be made perfectly. Our uniforms had to be clean and fit properly. Remember when I said the clothes they issued us were too big and flopped around on us? Well, after a few washings of this fine olive drab material they shrunk to a perfect fit. Our rifles had to be oiled properly and free of any rust. Our boots had to be shined to a high polymer shine.

It seemed like all those things were secondary if you had a clean and really shiny floor.

A shiny floor usually cancelled out any minor gigs. A gig was what they called a black mark on your platoon's record.

The Army had an unwritten point system for inspecting barracks. If your barracks had too many gigs they would confine the whole platoon to the company area, depending on the severity of your "gigness." (Hey, they can make up words, so I made this one up.) "Confined to the company area" meant just that. You couldn't leave the company area, which transfers to no beer hall and, unfortunately, no beer. The first platoon was always first. The third platoon was always second, and the second platoon was always third. I was in the second platoon; we were always last.

A bunch of my fellow soldiers got together and decided we had to do something about this. We all pitched in and put in extra hours cleaning our barracks. We spent the majority of the extra time on our floor. It looked like a mirror. The following weekly inspection produced the same result. The first platoon was first, the third second, and we were third again. We had to come up with a better plan for the next week. Extra humping didn't help. Humping is not an off-color word. It means "really working hard."

Charlie C. called for a secret meeting between five of us. He said, "I have a great idea," in his very strong Oklahoma accent. He said, "Have any of you seen that mangy dog loafing around here?" We all said that we had seen him. We figured it was a stray. Charlie said, "Now, we have to draw straws."

I thought to myself, "What's this screwball

up to now?" We drew straws, and Charlie drew the short one.

"S--t, I was afraid I'd draw the short straw."

Charlie used the word "s--t" often. Now he would have to go looking for it. Charlie's idea was to follow the dog when he saw him and wait until it defecated. He would then get a good sample of the dog's doo-doo.

When Charlie came back from his excursion he said, "I had to follow Fido for eight blocks until his time was right, and when he did finally go, he got mad at me, growled, and tried to bite me in the rear when I tried to pick it up."

Our plan was to go to the third platoon the night before the weekly inspection, carefully enter and rub the doo-doo on their usually perfectly shiny, pristine floor. The day after inspection everyone in the first platoon accused us of putting the doggie doo on their floor.

Charlie said, "It was probably that stray dog. Your perfect floor must have appealed to him."

The guy he was talking to said, "I wonder why that dog took the time to rub his doo-doo over our floor?"

Of course we were accused of doing this dirty deed. They figured, who else could it have been? Our whole platoon was confined to the company area for three days, because no one would fess up. Charlie acted stupid, but he wasn't. That was why we had a secret meeting. When they were trying to find out who did this, the five of us all acted as if we knew nothing.

The Gas Chamber

Our first training class was the "Gas Chamber." There were always rumors floating around about everything. Most of these rumors were pretty scary. Of course they had one about the Gas Chamber. I heard that one guy nearly died in the infamous chamber. Boy, I was not looking forward to this.

First, they showed us the proper use of the gas mask. Then they instructed us what to do if we were under attack of poisonous gas. I would put this situation on the same level as me running around in a jungle. It was not gonna' happen.

There was a procedure we practiced about 100 times. If we were attacked with gas we had to first put our rifles between our legs. We then had to put our helmets on top of the barrel of our rifles and then take our gas mask off our belts and attach it to our faces. We then had to put our helmets back on our heads, and we had to do all of these moves in thirty seconds. I think that is why we practiced it so much. They took us six at a time into the gas chamber with our masks off. There were three soldiers in this room already. They told us they were going to release gas from some canisters in a few minutes. I suppose it wasn't poisonous because there would have been some dead bodies lying on the floor already.

They said this little exercise was to let us feel how the gas would affect us. Hey, they could have told me what happens and I would have believed them. They said once the gas was released we had to stand there for at least thirty seconds. As an incentive they said if we tried to leave we would not eat for three days. Hunger can be a good motivator, so I thought I may try to stick this out. There was a huge second timer on the wall that started after the gas was released. One of the trainers turned the valve open on this supposedly non-fatal gas. Gee, I hoped it wasn't fatal. My eyes immediately began to burn and tears ran down my face. Wait, was I crying, or was I dying? I did the thirty seconds, but it wasn't easy. After the thirty seconds was up, five of us ran out of the chamber as quickly as we could. One idiot stayed an extra ten seconds. I guess he was trying to get brownie, or greenie, points. Oh, by the way, the three instructors had their masks on the entire time of this exercise.

A photographer was available to take pictures for our special edition "Army Basic Training book." That's just what I needed, a remembrance of all of this. The photographer got a good shot of Dick and Darryl holding hands and crying coming out of the chamber. If the Army didn't know these guys were gay, they should have known then.

Well, I got out of this alive and we went back into formation. In case you didn't know, a formation is when we line up in perfectly straight lines. The Sarge was standing in front of the formation telling us what a great job we did in this exercise. He then asked who had the best company. We all yelled in unison, "D-4-2, Sergeant!" He said, "Louder!" We repeated in a louder tone, "D-4-2, Sergeant!" In the back of the formation Corporal Heinz was throwing a few gas canisters into the formation. That D-4-2 crap was just a ploy. They wanted to distract us, and see how well our training sunk in.

My eyes began to burn the same as when I was in the gas chamber.

Everyone in the formation went through the gas mask drill except one guy, Private Wentz. I guess the poor guy panicked. When someone yelled, "Gas!" he threw his rifle up in the air and ran like hell. When the rifle came down, it landed on a few guy's heads. They received a couple of nice knots on their heads because they were in step three of the gas mask drill; their helmets were still on the barrel of their rifles.

The Sarge told Private Wentz to report to the front of the formation and go through the gas mask drill. He did it quite fast. Of course, the gas had dissipated by now. The Sarge said, "Congratulations Private, you did that quite well. You did it so well that you will be doing it every day and night until if, and when, you graduate from Basic Training. You will wear that gas mask twenty-four hours a day. You'll wear it when you're eating, sleeping, showering, and going to the Latrine. Latrine was another fancy army name for the men's room.

The Sarge told Wentz to remember these two words, "Wentz, gas! When you hear these two words you will immediately practice your gas mask drill." The Sarge would exercise this penalty to Private Wentz twenty to thirty times per day. The poor guy was a nervous wreck by the time eight week of training was over.

PT - Physical Training

Finally there was a word that makes sense:

training. It was quite physical. When I entered the Army on 1-9-63 I weighed 160 pounds. I was a fatty 160 pounds. When I was discharged on 1-8-65 I weighed 180 pounds. It was a solid 180 pounds. I now weigh 275 pounds. Needless to say there are not too many solid parts on my body today.

We arose at 0530 every morning. The prelude to the PT was usually a one mile or more run. We ran in our t-shirt and underwear, and of course, our boots.

In Augusta, Georgia, the temperature in the morning is anywhere from thirty to forty degrees. In the afternoon the temp' is between eighty and ninety degrees. I used to freeze every morning of these runs. It's funny though that I never got a cold.

Regardless of what I thought, the runs must have had some redeeming value. After the first time we ran I thought we were done and going back to eat breakfast. I was wrong. We lined up behind our barracks and did PT.

As I mentioned before, Corporal Heinz was a jerk, but he was in excellent physical shape. He led the PT exercises for about thirty to forty minutes. We did jumping jacks, push ups, and a bunch of other things I can't remember. I thought I was going to die right there. Just when I thought we were done we had to go to the "Monkey Bars." It beats me why they were called "Monkey Bars." The monkey bars were a structure of four 8x8 pieces of lumber with about twenty steel rungs stung about a foot apart. The structure was about eight feet off the ground. The sweet Corporal told us we had to do the whole length of the bars and then we could go to breakfast. What planet was he from? The first time I tried it I did four rungs and gave up. I went to the end of the line with the other failures, waiting to try again. This went on for about forty-five minutes. The Army always used food as a leverage tool and it usually worked. I was the last one to complete all the rungs. At the end of the eight week training I was doing the bars three times forward, and three times backwards. Yes, I said backwards; I was a maniac monkey bar freak.

The next morning at 0330, I heard a bunch of idiots running and screaming "Airborne." I asked a guy who was also awakened who the hell they were. He explained they were the airborne division of the Army. Their company was a few blocks from ours. He said that their training was a lot more vigorous than ours and that they made more money than us because they got paid every time they jumped out of an airplane. He also said that we all had the option to transfer to the airborne division for up to our third week of training. I thought to myself, "More money means more money to buy beer." I considered transferring over until I had a chilling thought. "Hey, I'm deathly afraid of heights." It took all my courage climbing that twelve-foot ladder just to paint that stupid Mess Hall. So much for the airborne division!

Hand-To-Hand Combat

Boy, this ought to be interesting. I was not much of a fighter. I got in a few fights when I was in grade school and a few in high school.

My Father died when I was nine years old.

I used to go to local fights with him, but he never taught me how to box. I wish I had learned. I watched a lot of studio wrestling when I was a kid. Eventually all the wrestlers would get their opponent in a head lock. That was basically wrapping your arm around your opponent's neck and squeezing until they gave up. So whenever I did get in a fight and my opponent held up his fists, I was usually screwed. I couldn't ask the guy to stand still while I wrapped my arm around his neck. Usually when I was trying to get a guy in a headlock he was beating the crap out of me with his fists.

The Sarge said he was going to pair us up in twos. "We will show you some hand-to-hand moves later on. I want you all to try to knock the crap out of your opponent the best you know how." I was hoping he would pair me up with one of the gay guys. I figured I had a good shot of whupping one of them.

Hey! This is better than I could imagine. My opponent was Joe J. You remember him, Mr. Peepers? He was about half my size and a little on the sissified side. He had to take his thick glasses off before we started. I thought to myself, "This is good. Now he wouldn't even be able to see me." I always wondered how he passed the eye exam part of the physical.

The Sarge blew his whistle signifying that we could start fighting. What does Mr. Peepers do? He gets in a classic boxing stance and raises his fists. Who would have thought the little jerk was a boxer. He proceeded to knock the crap out of me until the whistle blew again. I think that was probably the lowest point of my two-year Army career. To add insult to injury he apologized for beating me up so bad.

After this little fiasco they showed us a lot of hand-to-hand combat moves. I couldn't believe there wasn't a headlock move among them. I figured this training would be good for beer hall and tavern fights.

The next day we went to the rifle range. Oh boy, they were going to give us some bullets.

The Rifle Range

I had never carried or fired a gun or rifle in my life. In fact, I thought when you fired a rifle the bullet went straight to the target. I didn't realize it had an arcing flight. We had about three hours of classroom training on firing our rifles and then we proceeded to the rifle range.

My buddy Ulysses was on the ground beside me when we fired at our targets. The targets looked like they were five miles away. Actually they kept changing the targets from 100 to 500 feet away. There were spotters behind us with binoculars. After you fired, they would tell you where your shot landed. The targets were separated by five circles, with the bull's-eye located in the center. The further you were away from the bull's-eye the less point value your shot was worth. The guys in the rifle range pit held a paddle with a number on them to record each of your shots. If you missed the target altogether, they held up a huge red flag. This was commonly referred to as "Maggie's Drawers." Why it was called that beats me.

When the spotter behind you saw a red flag in front of your target he would yell, "Maggie's Drawers." I think they enjoyed hollering that. I would hear "2, 1, 2, bull, 3," and then he would scream, "Maggie's Drawers." I heard it a few times that day. But I could here Ulysses' spotter scream Maggie's Drawers at least fifty or sixty times. Poor Ulysses could not hit the side of a barn. He kept asking his spotter when he said Maggie's Drawers if he was sure.

The spotter would say, "Of course I'm sure."

The next morning after our PT training, we had a special formation to receive our rifle range scores. There were three classes of scores, marksmen, sharpshooter, and expert. The Sarge would say your last name first, and your first name last. He would then give you your numeric score and your class.

I'll use myself as an example. Folino, Edward, 180, sharpshooter. He went through a few other names and then got to Ulysses. He said, "Green, Useless." Ulysses blurted out, "Excuse me Sergeant, that's Ulysses." The Sarge said, "It's going to be Useless after you hear your freaking score. You fired a 12 out of a possible 250. You failed to qualify. You and Folino, see me in my room after this formation."

Nobody was ever called into the Sarge's room. It was like going to the Principal's office. Ulysses and I entered the Sarge's holy sanctuary. With his reputation I expected to see empty beer cans all over the place. His room was immaculate. Not a thing was out of place. I was impressed.

The Sarge said, "We have a problem here.

Did you know that everyone in the Company must qualify on the rifle range? If even one soldier does not qualify the whole Company will have to repeat the eight weeks of training over again. I don't think I can handle another eight weeks of you guys. I also don't think your fellow soldiers would appreciate going through another eight weeks of training with or without you guys."

He looked at me and said, "You and Green are relatively the same size. I want you to qualify on the rifle range again tomorrow."

I said, "Again?"

"Shut up. Wear Green's shirt with his name on it. You fired sharpshooter your first time. You don't have to get fancy. Just so you qualify."

I thought to myself again. "Ulysses was a black man from Augusta, Georgia. I was a greasy white Italian man from Pittsburgh, Pennsylvania." The Sarge must have known somebody at the rifle range. I didn't think any instructor would believe my name was Ulysses S. Green. Well, it worked. I fired a 225 for Ulysses, Expert. The Sarge thanked me. I guess we dodged that bullet.

Sunday Mass

I couldn't believe they let us go to church.

"You guys have one hour to walk to and do whatever you do at your church. There is a beer parlor on the way to the church area. If I find out somebody stopped at St. Hop & Barley you'll never get a weekend pass for the rest of your time here," the Sarge said.

There were about thirty of us from our

platoon who went to Mass. The beer parlor looked tempting, but I remembered what the Sarge said.

I entered a huge church. The Priest in this church was a Priest, a Chaplain, and a Colonel in the Army. For this Mass he was a Priest. The Mass was similar to the one I attended back home, until the sermon. As the priest approached the pulpit he screamed, "You're pigs, you're thieves. You'd steal your fellow soldier's underwear if you thought you could get away with it."

I assumed his sermon was going to be about stealing. In the Army, there are two classes of people: enlisted men and officers. The enlisted men were peons and officers were the hierarchy. They had their own mess hall, pools, and beer clubs. They were called the Officer's Club.

Well, even in church they had their own section. The Post Commander, a General, sat with his family in the first row. All the lesser officers would sit in the rows behind them.

The priest ended his sermon on stealing and then focused his attention on the General. He looked at the General and said, "I can't believe that you would transfer me to Vietnam when I only have a year to go until my retirement." You could see the General was shocked.

He then continued blasting the General about as many negative things about him that could come out of his mouth. This was hilarious. It dawned on me that he was acting as a priest now and not a soldier. Anyway, what could the General do to him? He already transferred him to Vietnam.

It was a very eventful Mass, but now I had to get back to do more soldiering.

Fireman

You'd think I would have learned my lesson about volunteering, but I did it again. We were standing in formation when the Sarge says, "Who wants to be a fireman?" I thought to myself again, "A fireman! My uncle and grandfather were firemen. I could use my training to try to get a job when I get out." I raised my hand as a few other suckers did too. Oh God, Dick and Darryl are volunteering too. Why would two gay guys want to learn how to be firemen?

The Sarge looked at the idiot volunteers and says, "Good, you will all report for training today at building 100. Your training will last two hours and you will all report back here when you are done."

I thought, "Two hours to learn how to be a fireman? Something fishy is going on here."

The future firemen and I report to this class. Our instructor says, "Hello class, so you want to be a fireman. Well, a good fireman must have good equipment to do his job efficiently." He reaches down on the floor and picks something up. He held it up in the air. It was a huge coal shovel. Unfortunately I knew what a coal shovel looked like. I used one in the fifties to shovel coal in my home's coal furnace. It's 1963 in Augusta, Georgia, and they still had coal furnaces.

In the Army, a Fireman was a stooge who stayed in the basement all night keeping a furnace fire going. Everyone else was sleeping real warm and cozy on the first floor. I can't believe how they suckered me in again.

Our instructor showed us how to start a fire, keep it burning, and put out a fire. He then told us something very scary. He said, "If you should fall asleep on fire duty, and your fire goes out, you can be court-martialed for it." Court-martial was another fancy name for, "We'll put you in the slammer." I thought, "That's just great!"

Somehow I was appointed to the "Head Fireman." My main job was to make the schedule for all the guys on fire duty. Being Head Fireman did have one distinctive advantage. It got me out of twenty-five mile forced marches. We took quite a few of those marches. Hey, that's what they called them. A forced march meant they forced you to walk twenty-five miles. Like you were going to say, "Sorry, I don't feel like marching today." Anyway, when these marches were scheduled, for some strange reason, I was on fire duty. Finally, volunteering had paid off for me.

The furnace room was smoky and cold. Although they had huge vents in the barracks upstairs, they expected me to sit or stand in front of the furnace for my heat. If I was too far away from the furnace, I was cold. If I got too close to the furnace, I was sweating. There was no in between. I would be in the furnace room until 0800 the next day. The forced march was scheduled for 0600, so I'm going to miss that. But I was still feeling sorry for myself. I think I was getting homesick.

There was one thing I did in basic training that I was not too proud of. While on the midnight shift, I would often write a letter home to my mom. It was three in the morning and I was trying to stay awake. I told my mom I was tired and cold and that everyone was telling me what to do. I told her they weren't feeding me enough and that I was sorry I ever volunteered for the draft. I told her I felt so bad that I may cry, and for affect I got some water and dropped a few drops on the letter.

Boy was I a jerk. I told my mom years later about adding the water to make it look like they were teardrops. She said, "You Stinker." Stinker. That's telling me, Mom.

My First Pay/Loan Sharks

When I was in the Army in 1963 we were paid once a month in cash. A finance officer was usually assigned to hand out the cash. He was always accompanied by an armed guard.

My pay as a Private E-1 was $78.00 per month and it had to last me a whole month. I needed to buy four movie theater tickets, at $0.50 each. I purchased four certificates for a hair cut at $1.00 per haircut since I had to keep my hair short at all times because of Army rules. They held back $37.50 a month for a $50.00 U.S. Savings bond. I needed at least $20.00 for the loan sharks. That left me with $15.00 for the month. All these expenses were necessities, especially the loan shark. They acted like your friends, but they were actually bloodsuckers.

Loan sharks usually operated as a team. One guy was the negotiator. He set the interest rates and I don't know why he set specific rates. With all loan sharks, the interest was the same. You had to pay back $7.50 for every $5.00 borrowed.

The due date was never negotiable. The loan sharks were standing outside the building after you were paid. They wanted their money right there. Remember I said there was a pair involved in loan sharking? The other half of the team was the enforcer. Need I say more? I will. He was usually six feet tall, or more, and two to three hundred pounds. He was also either a boxer, a wrestler, or just a guy that liked to beat up people.

When I was short of cash I would write home to my mom for a little donation. She usually came through for me. If it weren't for her I would have gotten a lot more knots on my head. Thank God for moms.

The Beer Parlor

I called them Beer Parlors. The Army called them the PX. PX meant "Post Exchange." I don't know why they didn't call it the PE?

The rumors were right. We didn't go to the Beer Parlor until the end of our third week.

Regular beer contained approximately seven percent alcohol. In the Army they served you 3.2 beer. That was 3.2 percent alcohol. You could still get drunk on it, but you had to drink twice as much of it to get the same effect as seven percent, or regular beer.

3.2 beer did make you pee a lot. When I drank it, it was painful. I would hold my bladder flow for as long as I could. I figured I would get drunker faster because the alcohol stayed in my blood stream longer. This was one example why I didn't pursue a medical career.

The only beer brand I recognized was Budweiser, but they also had Burgermeister, Lone Star, and others I had never heard of. Most beers have a yellow or orange color to them. I remember that the Lone Star beer was green. They should have marketed this beer as a laxative. It went through you so fast you might as well just sit on the toilet when you drank it.

Drinking a lot of beer usually causes a lot of gas. All American men have always been proud of the noise and nasty smell they can produce when passing gas. It is a very competitive thing. I wrote a poem for my third book called, "The Smell King." It is literally the history of me passing gas.

This first night of drinking there were eight of us there for five hours. It got pretty nasty. We would see if any one of us could drive someone away from the table from the natural act of passing gas.

One guy at the table was JD. His first name was John, and his last name was a long Hungarian name no one could pronounce. So, we all called him JD. I remember he was from Tiffin, Ohio. He told everyone at the table he had quite a reputation back in Tiffin when it came to passing gas.

I told him I was no slouch. I gave him a few of my best ones. He said, "Not bad, but get ready for this." All of his gas passings were SBDs: "Silent, but deadly."

I waited a few seconds and I couldn't believe what happened next. I got a shooting pain in my eyes and the top of my head. My head! I never got a shooting pain in my head before from a gas passing. As the tears ran down my face I did everything in my power to continue to sit there.

I said, "You're the Champ," as I got out of there for some fresh air. Thank God he lived in Ohio. I couldn't compete with something like that in Pittsburgh. Boy, it's funny what things guys will do while sitting around drinking beer.

Sick Call

Sick call was the Army term for going to see a Doctor. Go figure. If you went to Sick Call, you were usually called a variety of nasty names. Malingerer, chicken, and jerk are the ones that come to mind.

It was about my sixth week of training and I kept back from going to Sick Call as long as I could. But, I was having problems. I would have terrible nightmares that would wake me up. Also, when I woke up I had severe pains in my legs. I decided to bite the bullet and go to Sick Call.

I don't like to badmouth doctors, but it seemed the Army got all the incompetent ones. If you went to a dentist they never filled a tooth; they just pulled them. I don't know if they even knew how to fill them. The medical doctors were pretty much the same. Oh, there were probably some good ones, but I never saw them.

I told the Sarge I wanted to go on Sick Call the next morning. He asked me what was wrong. I told him it was personal. I can't believe he accepted that. He told me where I was to report to the next morning.

The Sick Call room accommodated about a hundred men. There were five or six rooms in the rear of the building where doctors were available. It all depended what your medical problem was as to which doctor you were sent to.

There was a huge sign in the front of the office that said, "Report here. Have your name, service number, and state your problem."

I approached the man under the sign. I gave him my name and service number. He said,

"Okay, what's your problem?"

I said rather sheepishly, "Nightmares." I was a little embarrassed.

He asked again, "What's your problem?"

I knew he heard me the first time. "Nightmares," I said louder.

He said rather loudly, "Nightmares!" Everyone in the room busted out laughing. I think this was a lower time in my army career than when Mr. Peepers beat the crap out of me.

The guy behind the counter conferred with two other guys. They were trying to figure out which doctor to send me to. They said in unison, "Dr. Rueben." I thought to myself, "Oh no, not another Psychiatrist."

It turned out he was a general practitioner. I sat in an uncomfortable folding chair for about two hours. Some of the other guys were looking at me and smirking. Well, no wonder, "Nightmares."

They finally called my name. I was told to report to Dr. Rueben, second door on the right.

The doctor seemed like a nice enough fellow. He said he had been working there for about two months, but that he never had to see anyone with chronic nightmares. I told him about my accompanying leg pains.

He said, "Do you drink a lot of beer?"

I said, "Every chance I can get." He thought for a second and said, I think I know your problem." When you go to bed at night the beer is settling in your legs and causing the pain.

I said, "Really," like I believed him.

He said, "I'm going to give you two prescriptions. One will be a large white pill to calm your nerves and curtail your nightmares. The other pill will be a small blue one. This one will help ease the pains in your legs. I want you to take the white pill an hour before you go to bed. I want you to take the blue one a half hour before you go to sleep."

I said, "Okay." As I was walking back to my barracks I thought of what he said about the blue pill. He said, "Take the blue pill a half hour before I go to sleep." I thought, "How the hell do I know when I'm going to go to sleep?" I could be laying there for ten minutes, or two hours. I figured I'd play it by ear, and see what happens. I took the pills for about three weeks. I couldn't believe it. They worked! Maybe the Doc knew what he was talking about.

Mail Call

Any soldier will tell you that the highlight of his day was "Mail Call." This term is self explanatory. The Army finally got one right.

There was nothing like getting a letter or package from home. For some reason, most letters were usually sent by women. I guess men thought it wasn't a manly thing to do. They were wrong. I think that trend has changed with all the sons and daughters we have fighting today in foreign countries. A letter from a father, brother, or dad would surely brighten any soldier's day.

One of the men would pick up our platoon's mail every day at 1100. I usually got two to three letters a week. My mom and a few aunts would write once a week. I never received mail from my uncles. See what I mean?

My mom would send homemade chocolate once in a while. It was so good I had to pace myself or I'd eat it all as soon as I received it.

My aunt Carmella sent me cashews quite a few times. I loved cashews, probably more than candy. She called them, "Cashoops." Hey, the Army had their words, and she had hers.

My Tattoo

Augusta, Georgia probably had ten tattoo parlors for every citizen. But very few of their citizens were getting tattoos. They were mostly there for the soldiers.

I always liked tattoos, so I decided to go get one in town. I decided I was going to get my tattoo before I got drunk. I saw a lot of guys get tattoos that they didn't want because they were drunk.

I went into a tattoo parlor, and since they all looked the same, I stopped at the first one I saw. It was called Eddie's Tattoos. How appropriate. Eddie was going to give a tattoo to Eddie.

Like most tattoo artists, Eddie had tattoos all over his body. He was something like a walking advertisement for his shop. He even had his name tattooed inside his lower lip. Boy that must have really hurt.

I liked roses. I saw a nice rose tattoo stencil, but didn't like the look of the leaves. Eddie said, "I can give you that tattoo for eight dollars. It's normally ten, but you don't want the leaves."

I said, "Okay, let me have that one then."

I didn't know getting a tattoo was painful. There is a motorized tattoo gun with a group of razor blades attached to the front of the gun. There was a tube for the tattooist to insert any specific color of ink.

Eddie applied a copy of the tattoo where I wanted it on my arm. The copies were something like the kids use today that are rub-off tattoos. He then turned on the tattoo gun. It vibrated up and down while cutting my skin. As it is cutting through to my skin the ink color is being fed in. I'll tell you, it was painful. It was something like sticking a pin needle in your arm. It hurts, but this hurt for about forty-five minutes, or until Eddie had completed the tattoo. Now I know why a lot of guys get drunk before they get a tattoo. Alcohol must have eased the pain.

When it was done, I liked it. I went to the barracks and asked the guys how they liked it. Hardly anyone knew what it was. One guy thought it was a flying saucer.

I said to myself, "I should have got those damn leaves." I went back the following weekend and had Eddie add the leaves on to my rose tattoo. More pain! I went back to my barracks, and everyone said, "Ah, it's a rose tattoo."

My tattoo is forty-six years old now, and it is quite faded. I went to a local tattoo parlor in Pittsburgh to see if I could get another tattoo to cover over my old one. The tattooist said, sure. It all depends on what size you choose. Our pricing starts at $150 to $400." I said, "$150! I only paid ten bucks for this one."

He said, "And that was how long ago?"

I said, "Forget it." I guess this tattoo is going to be with me when I die.

Memorable Moments

Joe J. was from Memphis. You remember him as Mr. Peepers who kicked my butt on the hand-to-hand combat exercise. Joe had spiked blond hair. Hey, it looked spiked. He had a real pale face. He was always writing mushy letters to girls. I know, I read a couple of them when he wasn't around. Boy, were they ever sickening.

Danny D. lived in Brookline, a few miles from where I lived. Danny had been married a couple of years. He was having some problems at home. I know because he discussed it with a few of us. When you eat, sleep, and work together every day and night, you are like family. What better people to ask advice from? Well, of course, none of us offered him any advice.

Joe J. must have overheard Danny discussing his problems with us. Do you know what he did? He wrote Danny's wife. He described himself as being six feet tall and Latin looking. Yeah, a five-foot-three blond-haired nerd was more like it. I wonder how he describes himself on the dating sites today?

Anyway, he told Danny's wife if she were ever in Memphis, he would like to take her out for a drink. He also told her he was a personal friend of Elvis. Danny's wife wrote Danny and told him about the letter Joe sent. Instead of getting mad, he was very amused. Elvis! Of course he did tell Joe if he wrote his wife again, he would kill him.

Monroe B. was a black guy from Alabama and he hated white people. Junior P. was white and from my home town of Beechview and he hated black people. They were always jawing at each other. Nothing ever turned physical, but that night it almost did. I guess the Sarge was out practicing his beer drinking. Junior came back from the beer parlor after probably drinking too many 3.2 beers and started hassling Monroe.

In the Army they have something called an entrenching tool. It was a really small shovel for digging foxholes. Foxholes were body-sized holes you dug to hide from the enemy. They also came in handy if someone was firing a round or two of bullets at you. That is, as long as you didn't stand up. Where the word fox fit into the equation, I didn't know. Well, Junior and Monroe decided they are going to fight each other with these little shovels. All of a sudden somebody yelled, "Not in here, you'll get blood on our shiny floor." They decided to go out to the back of the barracks. About twenty or so of us followed behind them. Then some guy had a premonition. He said, "They may kill each other." Why didn't I think of that?

It took four or five of us to keep them apart. We told them of this smart guy's premonition. They realized he might be right. They sort of shook hands, but they still hated each other. Where was the chaplain when you needed him?

Like I mentioned earlier, Billy C. was a real character. He never took anything seriously. He had one of those faces where he always looked like he was smiling. We got our first weekend pass and he asked me if I wanted to go home with him for the weekend. He said, "I have seven brothers and four sisters, and my mom loves to cook."

"Absolutely," I said. The thought of food that didn't gag me was the determining factor.

During my two years in the Army I always tried to visit as many different states as I could. Billy and I took a bus to Chattanooga. We arrived there on Saturday at 1500. There was a Moose Club across the street from the bus station and Billy was a regular customer there.

"Let's stop in for a beer, and I'll see if one of my friends is there and we'll find out if we can get a ride to my house," Billy told me.

In Tennessee they sold this beer called "Country Club." It was my first experience drinking malt liquor. Remember the beer parlor beer was 3.2% alcohol and regular beer was 7% percent alcohol. Well, Country Club was 12% alcohol. It was beer, but they called it malt liquor. Go figure. I don't remember what happened after the ninth or tenth beer, but I guess I had a good time. Billy woke me up at 0800. I was sleeping on a couch in the living room. He said, "Wow did you get screwed up. Anyway, it's time to eat."

You would not believe the spread that Billy's Mom put out. There were eggs, sausages, bacon, grits, fried potatoes, biscuits and gravy, toast, and pork chops. Yeah, pork chops. There were fourteen of us at this huge table in the dining room. Billy said that this was not a special breakfast. He said they ate like that every morning. Maybe that was why he was smiling all the time.

After breakfast we went back to the Moose.

Several hours later Billy woke me up from the back room and said, "Come on ole' buddy, it's time to catch our bus back to the Post." I guess I must have had too much to drink again.

When I got back a couple guys asked me

how I liked Chattanooga. I told them it was a very nice city, even though all I really saw was the Moose Club.

Jimmy M. was a black man from Florida. He was always being told about wearing his cap calked off to the side. He didn't know it then, but he was creating a fashion statement for many black men way back in 1963. But, it would take about forty years to catch on. Jimmy had a lot of girlfriends and a wife. He constantly was receiving x-rated mail from his girlfriends. Whenever he would get one he would read it to the whole platoon. It was the highlight of our day. I asked him why he never read us any mail from his wife. He told me he couldn't do that. They were too personal.

Gary G. was from Dallas, Texas. His last name was Greasenhimer. For simplicity sake Sarge called him "Grasshopper." Gary was a strange looking fellow. He had a long thin face with a hook nose. He had a five o'clock shadow at 0900 in the morning, even though he shaved two hours before. About the sixth week of our training Gary flipped out. We thought he was going crazy. His eyes were going up his head and he was slobbering. One of the guys there said he knew what was happening. He said Gary was having an epileptic seizure. We were bewildered how he passed an Army physical. They transferred Gary to another company where they could watch him. The Sarge told Gary that it would take from eight to ten weeks to process him out of the Army. Why so long? Hey, we're talking about the Army.

My basic training was in Ft. Gordon, Georgia. I returned to Ft. Gordon for Army Signal School.

I saw a guy from my old platoon one day and I asked him what happened to Gary.

"Are you ready for this? He's still in that company they transferred him to, but he's on a special detail." Detail was an Army name for work, or a job. The guy continued. "Gary is guarding an ammo dump." An ammo dump is where they store live ammunition like bullets, bombs, grenades, and any other explosives.

I asked, "Did they give him a loaded rifle?"

"Yes, do you believe that?" he replied.

I couldn't believe it. "He's an epileptic! Do they even know that?"

"Hey, this is the Army. I'm sure they do."

This was pretty unbelievable to me.

I don't have much to say about Dick and Darryl except they seemed to somewhat enjoy their eight weeks of training. I'm sure they're married by now, living in San Francisco, and telling their grandkids about what they did in the war.

Ulysses and I received our first weekend pass after our fourth week of training. We decided to check out Augusta, Georgia. It was a Saturday. Ulysses did not drink alcohol. It took all my will power not to drink when we went to town. I figured I could go back on Sunday and get plastered. I was about to get a culture shock. Ulysses was from Macon, Georgia, and had seen this before. Most of the restaurants had a black entrance and a whites-only entrance. I was shocked. It turns out that I could eat in the black section, but he couldn't eat in the white section.

He said, "I thought you knew about this."

I said, "No, I did not." I asked him if he wanted

to go back to the Post and eat. He said that was okay with him. I'd say we have come a long way since that Saturday in Augusta, Georgia, 1963.

Vic J. was from Brookline, the same area as Danny D. Each platoon elected a squad leader. There were usually fifteen to twenty in a squad and Vic was elected our leader. Vic liked to drink like the rest of the Pennsylvania guys. I guess it must have something to do with our steel mills. Vic would hooch it up every night and he always had a hard time getting up in the morning.

The squad leader was what it implied. He was your leader. After about a week of squad leading, Vic was out later than usual one night. I tried to wake him up for about fifteen minutes the next morning but he would just mumble and go back to sleep. I saw the Sarge coming down the side aisle and I noticed Vic was still in his bunk. I told him the Sarge was coming and that he had better get up. He just mumbled again.

The Sarge got to Vic's bunk and asked me, "What's the matter with him?"

I said "I think he has a bad cold."

The Sarge said, "It smells like he tried to cure himself with alcohol." He grabbed the center of Vic's bottom sheet and lifted him up expecting him to land prostrate on the floor. Then the most amazing thing happened. While Vic was in mid air he managed to land on his two feet and say, "Good morning Sarge. How are you today?" I couldn't believe what he had done. The Sarge looked at him with a grin on his face. He told Vic he should have been out of that bunk fifteen minutes ago. Vic was replaced that day as our squad leader.

There was a great deal of prostitution in Augusta, Georgia. We all had to attend a class on venereal disease but we had mail call first.

I could see Charlie C. across from me reading a letter. He really looked upset. I could have sworn he was crying. I wondered if he had gotten a "Dear John Letter." A Dear John letter was a letter from a girlfriend telling you that she didn't want to be your girlfriend anymore. Unfortunately, some married guys got Dear John's from their wives. I guess after a few weeks these girlfriends and some wives realized they were better off without their beaus.

I asked Charlie what the problem was. He said he didn't want to talk about it. The whole platoon went to a small room to see a film on venereal disease. Right after the film started there was a blood curdling scream. The lights were turned on immediately. There was Charlie screaming uncontrollably. The Sarge ran over and calmed him down a little. And I went over to see if I could consol Charlie. I asked him what the problem was. He said he received a Dear John letter from his girlfriend's mother.

"Her Mother!" I said to him.

"Yeah, she said I'm too old for her daughter."

Charlie and I were both seventeen. I asked Charlie how old his girlfriend was. "Twelve and a half. Almost thirteen."

"Charlie, maybe she is a little young for you."

"Yeah, maybe you're right. She has a sister that's fifteen years old. Maybe her mom will let me write her."

"Yeah, maybe," I told him.

Graduation

The whole Company had to take a PT test at the conclusion of our training. The major part of this test included going through an obstacle course. We had practiced on this course plenty of times. We practiced it until every one in our platoon could complete it. Dick, Darryl, and Mr. Peepers practiced it the most and it paid off in that they completed it.

Sarge was ecstatic. He said, "You bunch of screw-ups surprised me. I'm almost proud of you. As a token of my appreciation I've bought beer for a little party." It was really a little party. Most of us had two beers, and the beer was gone. So of course most of us decided to go to the beer parlor and have a real party.

I knew Ulysses didn't drink, but he would have enjoyed this party, from what I remember of it. A few weeks earlier, Ulysses experienced shortness of breath. An examination discovered a heart murmur. See, they did have some good doctors. He received a medical discharge and was immediately sent home. I was sorry to see him go. My new bunkmate was none other than Mr. Peepers, who I'm glad didn't come to our party.

I don't recall coming back from the beer parlor. I woke up with a burning in my chest. I thought, "Oh God, I'm having a heart attack." I wasn't. My wool blanket and sheets were on fire. I had fallen asleep with a cigarette in my hand.

In 1963 you were allowed to smoke in the barracks. I heard a bunch of guys screaming. There was Mr. Peepers in the bunk below me sheepishly yelling, "Fire, fire," in his very timid voice. There were little pieces of flame falling down on him, but he wouldn't get out of his bunk. He kept yelling, "Fire, fire." Somebody pulled him out of his bunk. I don't remember who. Meantime, I'm just as bad as Peepers. I'm still laying in the smoldering blanket, sheet, and mattress. Charlie and a few other guys ran over and threw me off the bed. I remember it was pouring down rain that night. Charlie grabbed the mattress, which by now had a huge hole in it. It was still smoldering. He took it outside figuring the rain would stop the smoldering. A couple guys took the blanket and sheets and put them in the latrine's sink. They ran water on them to stop the smoldering. I went out to the back of the barracks and tried to bring the mattress back inside. A couple of guys stopped me, and returned the mattress to the pouring rain. I guess I went back to the barracks and fell asleep on my bed springs. This was all told to me the next morning. I don't remember anything about that night, except thinking I was having a heart attack.

I woke up in the morning sleeping on a set of springs. It was very uncomfortable. Charlie filled me in as to what happened. "After we took the mattress out in the rain you went out and tried to bring it back in. Of course, we stopped you. It was still smoldering. We talked you into going back to your bunk. You didn't even notice that you didn't have any blankets or sheets on your bunk. You just laid there on the springs." The good news is the Sarge must have slept through the whole thing. He must have been celebrating getting rid of us.

We were told to turn our sheets and blankets

into the supply department and then report to a formation behind the barracks. In the supply room there was a pile for the sheets, and a pile for the wool blankets. Everyone was throwing them to their respective piles. I had mine folded neatly and placed them on the right piles. I didn't want the supply Sergeant to see the burns on my stuff. He looked at me strangely but said I could go. We were also told to fold our mattresses in thirds on our bunks. I folded mine so the hole in the middle of it did not show. I waited until Mr. Peepers went out back for the formation. I then switched his good mattress with my burnt one. Wow, was I genius or what?

For some strange reason, the formation was delayed about an hour. The reason was to find out our MOS, and where we would be transferred to from Ft. Gordon. MOS meant: "Military Occupational Specialty." There were numerous MOS's. For example there was infantry, signal corp, finance, security, and so on.

The Sarge would say your name, your MOS designation, and where you were to report to after your two week furlough. Furlough was the Army's name for a vacation. When the Sarge got to my name he didn't give my MOS, or where I was to report after my furlough. He said, "Folino, Edward, report to the Supply Sergeant."

I thought to myself, "Oh my, I think I'm in trouble." I was in trouble.

The Supply Sergeant had figured out my little scam. He looked at my sheets and blankets after I left his building. He must have gone to my barracks and figured out I switched the mattresses. The Supply Sergeant told me I had to pay for all the government property I destroyed. It would be taken from my pay each month until the full amount was paid. The Army garnished my pay for six months. I think I paid for that mattress, sheets, and wool blanket ten times over. I knew it wouldn't do any good to complain. I'm just lucky they didn't court martial me. I did manage to requisition (steal) a wool blanket before I was discharged. I still have it forty-three years later. I use it to line the trunk of my car. Justice is served.

Epilogue

All in all basic training was a good experience for me. I met a lot of good men, and had a lot of memorable experiences. I also learned to control what little money I received every month. This was good practice for when I received unemployment checks after I got discharged.

There were some men from my Company that volunteered for a three year term. A lot of them went to Vietnam and never returned. For that, I am truly sorry. I pray every day for the men and women who are fighting for our country today.

I'd like to dedicate this story to Charlie Couey. About five years ago I received a telephone call while watching a Steelers playoff game.

My wife said, "There's a strange phone call for you. I can't understand him. He has a strong southern accent. I think his name may be Charlie." The only thing I remembered at the time was who the hell would be calling me during this game.

"Hi Ed, it's Charlie," the voice said.

"Charlie who?" I said.

"Charlie Couey."

Then I remembered him. I said, "Charlie, you old son of a gun. How did you find me?" He told me he found me through a search on the internet.

I said, "I'm watching the Pittsburgh Steelers playoff game."

He said his favorite team was the Dallas Cowboys and I told him they weren't bad, but I had to root for the home team, my Steelers.

Charlie said that he was calling all his old friends, including the ones he knew from the Army. Charlie told me he was happy that I still remembered him. He asked if I remembered all the weird things we did and he went over all of them. I told him that I'd never forget any of them, or him.

I could tell something was on his mind. I said, "You didn't receive a Dear John letter again, did you?"

He sort of laughed and said, "Oh you remember that too." He then told me he had an inoperable brain tumor, and less than six months to live. He also told me he had been to three doctors and that they all gave him the same diagnosis.

I felt really bad. An old friend had found me and now I was losing him. I assume Charlie is dead now. After the doggie doo incident, Charlie said to me, "You know Ed, some day someone should write a book about all the crazy stuff we did in Basic Training." So I did. Here you go Charlie. I hope you liked it.

THE BIG HEIST

(I'm going to tell this little story from
the point of view of a ten year old.)

My friend Dewey was three years older and
I idolized him. He had all kinds of skills that I didn't
have. He could make anything with an erector set
– a car, any kind of building, anything. You name it
and he could build it. He taught me how to make
homemade firecrackers. I made one at home one
day and it blew up in my hand. I was lucky. I put
my hand in ice water for about three hours. My
mother never knew what happened. That was the
last of my bomb making adventures.

Dewey knew how to play the guitar. I had
a hard time whistling. Dewey had his own gang,
of which he was the head of. I guess you could
call me an honorary member. I was younger than
Dewey and the other kids in the gang. I think they
just tolerated me because I went to school with
Dewey's sister.

Dewey had another skill. He was a master
thief. The closest thing I got to being a thief was
taking a dime out of my mom's purse for a bottle
of Yahoo.

The gang had a hideout in the basement
of a neighbor's house up the street from where
Dewey lived. We had to make sure no one was
around, and then we would remove a wooden
grate and enter into our little house of iniquity. The
hideout was well equipped. It contained pillows,

blankets, a couple of lamps, and the customary girlie magazines. Dewey tapped into the guy's electric cable to provide us with our power. See, I told you he was smart. The guy who owned the house was old, probably fifty-five, and he was hard of hearing. It was a perfect set-up.

Dewey told me he was working on a big job and he was going to let me help. He said the plans were almost complete and I was to meet him at the hideout on the following Saturday afternoon. I thought to myself, "Geez. I hope it's just a little robbery and we weren't going to bump somebody off." I didn't think we hated anybody bad enough to kill them, so I erased that thought from my mind.

Now, to the matter at hand. It was a robbery, thank God.

Dewey passed out small spiral notebooks to all of us. He said he stole them from the last heist. Boy, this friend of mine was a real thinker. The heist was to be on the following Saturday at the Murphy's, not far from Dewey's house. Every one of us had a letter designating who they were. I was E-2 because we had another Eddie in the gang, E-1. At the top of the first page in red was "Murph-26." I didn't want to act stupid but I thought that might have meant the gang robbed Murphy's twenty-five times already. I thought to myself, "This is going to be easy. They've robbed this place twenty-five times already and haven't been caught."

Dewey cased the Murphy's a couple times during the week. By the way, the Saturday we did this heist was the day before Mother's Day. I felt a little guilty, but I thought Dewey would give me some money and I could buy my mom a nice gift at Murphy's. Heck, maybe that's what we were going to do: steal Mother's Day gifts. No chance. We were going to steal pen knives and candy bars. Dewey had orders for the knives from his school. The kids weren't allowed to buy them because they were too young. The candy was for the hideout. Dewey was going to steal the knives and I was going to get the candy. I was excited because I got a key job on my first heist.

When Dewey cased the Murphy's, he wrote down all kinds of important information. The plan was for us to do our stealing while the other guys occupied the clerks helping them with Mother's Day gifts that Dewey knew they didn't have. Dewey went over everything with us. He told the other guys that we only needed about five minutes or less to get our booty.

Well, the big day came and everything went according to plan. That was surprising because my legs were like Jell-O and I could hardly walk. I said a short prayer that everything would go right and that none of us would get caught. Pat cleaned out all of the knives but I only got four candy bars. One of the sales clerks abandoned E-1 and was walking toward me and I got the heck out of there.

Dewey yelled at me when we got back at the hideout. He told me I was out of the gang because I almost got caught. I tried to blame it on E-1, but he didn't want to hear it. I asked him if he could give me a couple of bucks so I could buy my mom a Mother's Day gift. He said, "I bet that you want to buy something at Murphy's." I said, "Sure."

He told me to get out and never go to Murphy's again. He never did give me any money. I decided to write my mom a poem. That always seemed to work and it didn't cost me anything.

I went to school the following Monday and started to have guilty feelings. Besides that, everyone was talking about the big heist at the Murphy's. I didn't go to the same school as Dewey, but I guess they were talking about it at his school too. Dewey attended one of those schools for brainy kids.

One of my buddies said, "That Murphy's has been robbed twenty-five times."

Like a jerk, I said, "No, twenty-six." I always did have a big mouth.

My buddy asked, "Hey, did you have anything to do with it?"

"No way, I'm not going to go to jail for a couple of knives and some candy bars." Oops, there I went again. I told my buddy not to say anything, but I knew that Dewey had robbed the Murphy's. I said he was bad news, and if you squeal on him I'm sure he would kick my friend's butt." He agreed to stay quiet. I hoped he didn't have a big mouth like you know who.

Our school had a church in the basement. I decided to go to confession and tell the priest about my crime. I figured I could use this as a back-up in case I got caught. I thought if I'm caught I could say, "I'm sorry, I even went to confession and told Father Mario what I did."

Father Mario was a new priest in our church. He was pretty young, and he was sent to our church to assist Father John who was pretty old. I know you're not supposed to tell what you tell in the confessional, but we're talking about my life here. When I told Father Mario what the gang and I did he told me I had two options. I could tell my parents what I did and have them go to the store and pay for the candy bars. Or, I could buy the candy bars somewhere else and go back to Murphy's and replace them. The second option sounded like a winner to me. I thanked Father Mario and was feeling good about myself until he gave me my penance. Penance was usually doled out according to the severity of the crime. I had heard the Father Mario was a fair man, but he wasn't that day. Father Mario told me I had to say fifteen rosaries, two-hundred Hail-Marys, seventy-five Our Fathers, and a thousand Glory be to the Fathers. I got a thousand Glory Be's because they were so short in length. I'm not a math genius but I figured I'd probably be a senior in high school when I completed saying all these prayers, that is, if II wasn't in prison. On top of all this marathon praying, I had to replace the stinking candy bars.

I bought the candy bars at a local store and prepared to go to Murphy's. It was a Tuesday night around five. The store was usually quiet at that time, because people were home eating their dinner. I went into the store and headed toward the candy counter. There was no one there, which wasperfect. I went to return the candy and a clerk jumped up from behind the counter and said, "Can I help you, son? Do you want to purchase those four candy bars? Hey, I recognize you. You were here last Saturday when our store was robbed and someone stole the last four Snickers bars that were on this display. I went to order more yesterday but my distributor was out of them. So where the heck did you get those four?"

I was trapped like a dog. I didn't know what to say. I was fumbling with my words when the clerk said, "I have a good deal for you. You pay for the ones you stole last week, give me those four, and never come back in here again."

He called this a good deal. I'd hate to see a bad deal. I agreed to his deal, though. You know they say, "Crime doesn't pay." Well they sure are right. I almost became a master criminal's assistant, almost got caught stealing twice, and I didn't even get a Snickers bar. What a bummer. My life of crime was over!

THE BLIND DATE... 1973

I was a real freak when it came to Elvis Presley. I had all of his records, I tried to comb my hair like him, and had a failed attempt to dress like him. My room at home had Elvis pictures glued all over the wall and ceiling. In the mix, I had one picture of Kim Novak and another of Bridget Bardot. I didn't want people to think I was gay or in love with Elvis in that kind of way.

I came home from work one day and my mom told me Elvis was coming to Pittsburgh. I thought to myself, "Man, I'd love to see him in person, but I know the tickets would be almost impossible to obtain."

Wouldn't you know it, my Aunt Sally called. "Eddie, how would you like to see Elvis Presley?"

I couldn't believe what I was hearing. I said, "Of course I would. How'd you get the tickets?"

She told me her husband, my Uncle Tom, who was a stagehand, was going to be working the show and managed to finagle a couple of good seats.

But then she dropped the bomb. She said, "There's a little catch."

"How little of a catch?" I asked.

She went on, "You have to take a friend of mine as your date, a blind date if you will."

I said, "I've never been on a blind date, but I've heard a lot of nightmare stories about them—what does she look like?"

She said, "She's kind of cute."

There was another phrase I didn't like to hear. I figured if she was that bad I just wouldn't talk to her that much, enjoy the show, and then take her home.

The history of my dating experience can be summed up in one word, "The Post-Gazette." Let me explain this to you. In 1973 I was an alcoholic, and I practiced my alcoholism when I went out drinking at night. When my friends and I went out boozing most of them would meet a chick (that's what we called them then) and take them home, or at least get their phone number to be called for a future date. Me, I was always so drunk the chicks didn't even want to talk to me, therefore that's where the Post-Gazette comes into play. I'd usually be the last one in the bar, and after closing, I would always stop and get a morning paper to take home with me. I was usually too drunk to read it by then, but at least I took something home.

Well, back to the infamous blind date. I received directions to my future date from my aunt. I figured with my track record I must be doing something wrong with the women I tried to hook up with. I was going to try a new approach. On the few dates that I went out on, I would always have six or seven drinks before I left the house. After six or seven more I was usually on my way to being blitzed, and my date would go home alone or with one of my so-called friends. I've been told I'm extremely shy, hence the over-drinking. It was going to be tough, but I left my house without taking a drink to meet my future kind of cute date.

She lived in a huge apartment building in Washington, Pennsylvania, right off route 79. Oh, another thing, I'm extremely afraid of heights. You know where her apartment was? The 46th floor.

I guess it would be rude of me to call and tell her to meet me in her lobby. I decided to take the death elevator up to the 46th floor. Thank God there were only a few windows on the floor and I kept away from them.

I knocked on her door and she answered with her robe on. She was kind of cute. I thought to myself, "Either she's not ready yet, or I'm going to get lucky before we leave for the show."

She said, "Hi, I'm Debbie, you must be Ed."

I felt saying, "Are you up to role playing? I'm the plumber, and I'm here to fix your leaky faucet." But she didn't look like she had a sense of humor, so I said, "Yes I am. Are ready to see The King of Rock and Roll?"

She said, "What an ego—does he really call himself that?" Strike One!

She told me she had to work overtime and that she got home late. She told me that we still had a lot of time and that I should sit in the living room while she got ready.

I pass a very small kitchenette on my way to the living room. The living room looked like a summer display room at Home Depot. All the furniture was the cheap nylon type you take to a pool or put on a crappy looking patio. I wondered what kind of furniture she had in her bedroom, not that I'd ever see the room or the furniture in it.

I was getting thirsty, so I yelled toward her bedroom, "Do you have anything to drink?" I figured one wouldn't hurt, and it would loosen my tongue a little.

She yelled back, "There's wine coolers in the refrigerator, help yourself. Don't touch the beer, that's for someone else."

I figured the beer was for some other loser she knew who didn't want to see Elvis. I had a wine cooler and boy, was it lousy.

She came out of her bedroom looking like a colossal mismatch of cotton, blue slacks, green top, and a ugly paisley sweater. Oh, and yellow patent leather high boots. I took a big gulp and said, "You look nice." I didn't know that only one wine cooler would let you lie like that.

We took the shaky elevator (I'm also afraid of elevators) down to the lobby and walked to get my car. I had a brand new 1973 black on black Ford Thunderbird with black leather interior, a real beauty if I don't say. I let her in the car, thinking she would say something about it. Everybody did—I guess cars didn't do it for her.

We were cruising down 79 not really talking about anything, and then she drops the bomb, "Can I ask you a personal question?"

I thought to myself, "What the hell can be personal? I don't even know you." But I said, "Sure, I'll answer your question."

"How much did you pay for this car."

I said, "$6,800," a lot of money back in 1973.

"Wow, you got robbed! That's a lot of money for this car. I like my Mustang much better."

I asked her what kind of car she owned and she told me she owned a piece of shit 1973 4-cylinder mustang with automatic shift. A real classic. Not! She didn't say, piece of shit, she said classic, I added the piece of shit part myself.

Similar to the old west, nobody talks about a man's horse, but today, nobody talks about a man's car. Strike two!

We arrived at our seats which, turned out to be pretty good. We were in the first row, first level seating and no one could sit in front of us. The show started and the King looked and sounded great. This was 1973, remember, before he looked like a butter ball. The guy beside me had some powerful binoculars, and I asked him if I could borrow them for a minute. After I took a few peaks at Elvis, Debbie asked me if she could borrow them to take a look. She looked

In the binoculars for a few minutes and then gave them back to the guy beside me.

She then looked at me and said, "I don't know what all the hullabaloo is—I don't even think he's that cute." (Hullabaloo meant fuss in the 70's.)

I was going to give her strike three on that statement, but I decided to leave the concert a little early and take her across the street to the U.S. Steel building. They had a lounge in the basement that was supposed to be a happening place.

I'm glad we bugged out of the concert early, otherwise we never would have gotten a table. I asked Debbie if she wanted a drink. I wasn't about to buy her food since she had been acting like a jerk and bad-mouthing my car and the King, twice.

She said, "I'll have a whiskey and ginger ale."

I ordered a whiskey and ginger ale for her and a triple whiskey and soda for myself. She didn't say a word—hey, maybe I will get lucky tonight. After she took a sip of her drink, I asked her how it was.

She said, "It's very strong"

I thought, "Is there no pleasing this woman?"

I called the waitress over and asked what kind of whiskey she served us. She said that I didn't specify, so she gave us Four Roses, the garbage whiskey of the 70's.

I told the waitress to throw away the first drinks and that I would pay for them, but to bring us a VO and ginger for Debbie and a VO and soda for me. After I saw Debbie take a sip of the VO, I asked her, "Well, how's that drink?"

She said, "I think it's the worst drink I've ever had in my life." Not, "It's not bad, it's too weak, it's still strong, but, it's the worst drink she ever had in her life." Strike three!

I looked at her and said, "Okay, we're out of here, right now," and I didn't say it in a nice way.

"We didn't see the band yet," she said.

I said, "You want to see the band, why, you wouldn't like them anyway. If you didn't like Elvis Presley, you're not going to like a band that just arrived here after practicing in one of their grandmother's garage. We're out of here."

We didn't speak at all for the trip to her place. I pulled up in front of her apartment building and said, "Okay, get out."

"Aren't you going to take the elevator with me and walk me to my apartment?" she whined.

"Walk you to your apartment? You're lucky I didn't leave you in the Steel Building!" I told her.

She got out of my inferior car and I drove to the Beechview Moose to get sloppy drunk. Maybe if I got a little drunk before I picked Debbie up, I could have handled her a little better.

The next day my aunt asked how my date with Debbie went. I didn't have the heart to tell her the fiasco it was. I just told her that Debbie just wasn't my type.

My Aunt Sally died a few years ago, and I almost told her a few times what a nightmare that night was. I guess after she reads this, she'll know. Sorry, Sal.

X-RAYS AND CHICKEN
(90 minutes on the South Side)

(Some people compare the South Side of Pittsburgh to New York's Greenwich Village, but the South Side does not have as much history as Greenwich Village. Most of the people from the Village are a little strange and the people from South Side are just Pittsburgh people.)

I was pretty sick for four days with a fever, persistent cough, and assorted aches and pains, so I decided to take a shot at my family physician. From all the coughing and germ spreading in the doctor's office, it looked like I was not alone with this dreaded disease. (The flu?) There was another open air "smoker's only" germ section outside of the doctor's office. It was nice of the nurse to squeeze us in, even though we didn't have an appointment. The doctor's verdict was fast and simple. I had a severe sinus infection which affected my ears, throat, lungs, balance, and more. Whatever it could affect, it did. I had to go to my pharmacy to get an antibiotic, and the good doctor gave me a complimentary nose spray to be used once in the morning and once at night. As a precautionary move, he wanted chest x-rays done at the hospital. The doctor told me to call him the following afternoon and he would give me my results.

My wife and I used to love Kentucky Fried Chicken, but since they came out with their new recipe, it seems tasteless. There is a Popeye's

69

down in the South Side near Wharton Square, so I figured I'd get my x-ray at the South Side Hospital and shoot over to get some chicken for dinner.

I didn't know where to park when I arrived at the hospital. It had been quite a while since I'd been there. Actually, the hospital building is there, but there are no patient rooms. It has outpatient services, a lot of offices, and a whole lot of, "I don't know" since it was taken over by UPMC. There were a few empty parking spaces right in front of the hospital so I parked in one of them. I put a quarter in the meter, which registered sixteen minutes. I only had three quarters with me so I deposited the other two making me legal for forty-eight minutes. There was a "Two hour only" limit on each meter. I guess that's why I saw a lot of couples or sets of twos there. One was there for hospital related business and one was there to keep feeding the parking meter. I thought to myself, "Maybe I'll be in and out of there in less than an hour." Then I thought to myself, "Sure. And chickens will begin to fly to the Arctic."

I entered through the main automatic door. Boy was this place clean. I saw a huge sign with an arrow pointing to the left that read, "Reception." I knew that would get me going in the right direction. I walked up to a huge reception station where an attractive 40-ish red haired woman was typing on a computer keyboard. I must have worn my invisible cologne because she never looked up for at least three to five minutes. I decided I would use my cough attention trick. That sort of backfired because I coughed for at least three minutes straight with everyone's attention except the receptionist. Evidently I didn't use the proper mouth covering technique in front of the experienced health care experts. She finally acknowledged me, thank God.

I handed "Red" a copy of the script for my x-ray and then asked if I was in the right place. She looked at me with utter contempt and said, "Yes." I think she was put out because evidently she had to enter all the application information in her computer for my chest x-ray. I thought that was her job though. She looked at the first line where my name was and said to me, "What is your name?" She had that same look of contempt. Hey it wasn't my fault that she couldn't read my doctor's writing. I told her my name and she asked if I had ever been to the South Side Hospital, which I had. When I told Big Red that I had, she said, "Then why can't I find you in the system?"

"Hey, I don't know," I told her.

"It's because they have it under Ed and not Edward," as if it was my fault.

I decided to try a different approach with this woman. I was going to be super friendly. I noticed she had a ring on every finger and both of her thumbs. The rings were the type you'd find at a flea market in the back aisle for two dollars, or three for five. It's a shame she had such junky rings because she had a beautiful shade of purple nail polish on her nails. I thought about complimenting her on the pretty shade of polish, but I thought she might think I was gay or that I was trying to make her. Complimenting her nail polish would be like her telling me she liked the smell of my cologne, which was never going to happen anyway. I asked if her finger nails got in her way when she was typing. I barely had the last word out when the look appeared again. She abruptly said, "Not at all." I just stood there for the next 5-7 minutes while she typed my admission form.

When she was done she printed my form and handed it to me. "Go to the Visitor's elevators down this hall, go to the second floor, and turn left out of the elevator, and go to the office that's marked Imaging." I wondered if I had enough time on my meter to get this done, so I asked Miss Personality how often the cars were ticketed around there. She said, almost in a civil tone, "It's a hit or miss type thing." I was going for the miss. I thanked my guardian angel, turned around, and headed for the elevators. She yelled, "No stu...," caught herself, and then said, "Down this hall to the elevators, sir," pointing at another hall. When she was telling me where to go for the x-ray I wasn't really listening to her. I was wondering about my parking situation.

I entered the visitor's elevator and pushed the button for the second floor. It seemed like forever getting up one lousy floor. The elevator had stopped and I was looking at a huge piece of shiny steel. I must have stood there at least a minute or two when I heard voices behind me. When I got on the elevator I was the only one on it. Was I on a haunted elevator? I turned around and observed people getting on. I then realized it was one of those elevators that you enter on one side, and then exit from the other side. Duh!

The two women at the imaging department were nice and professional. I was in and out of there in under ten minutes. I thought about stopping at Red's desk and telling her she should have told me about the elevator situation, but I figured she'd just laugh at me. As I passed near her desk, I waved and said, "Catch you later."

I detected a very small movement coming out of the corner of her mouth, and then she said, while back in the contempt mood, "You too."

I arrived at my car with six minutes to spare. Now it was time to go on to Popeye's Chicken for a 9-piece to go. I also always ordered a chicken wrap to eat in the car. I would sit in my car, eat my wrap and just people watch. When I worked in New York City, I lived on 42nd street. If I ever became bored in my room I would go out on the sidewalk, stand there, and people watch. NYC had its share of wackos, plus some. Wharton Square on the South Side wasn't as bad as NYC, but it was getting pretty close to it.

I sat in my car and prepared to eat my chicken wrap. A car pulled up beside me with a radio so loud I could have heard it on my back porch five miles away. Three people, if you want to call them that, emerged from this mobile stereo SUV, two guys in their twenties, and a young girl wishing she were in her twenties. I'd say she was around fifteen or sixteen. Her mini, mini skirt was so short that if she blew her nose she would have been arrested for public exposure. I won't even get into her see-thru top. One guy got back in the car, so I couldn't critique his attire. The other one you would not believe. Do you know the style today in which the guys advertise underwear, which they proudly wear on the outside of their jeans? Of course you do. Well this guy had on two pair on the outside of a pair of black jeans that were worn about ten inches up from his knees. From where I was sitting in my car I could see through the front window of the store when the double underwear dodo tried to sit in a chair. He had to sort of lay back and hold on to the sides of the chair. His underwear were so tight he couldn't bend over to sit down. This scene reminded me of a Seinfeld show where Kramer had on a pair of jeans on that were so tight he couldn't sit down. Funny stuff!

It was time to go home to Mt. Washington and some normalcy. I usually end my stories or tales with a surprise ending of some sort. I think there was enough lunacy in this little short story to forgo that procedure. Oh yea, the young girl who went into the Popeye's had a nice shade of green hair with streaks of purple going through it – priceless.

BLINKY
FIVE YEARS LATER

Hi, my name is Blinky and I appeared in a poem in Ed Folino's first book of poetry, "Long Time Coming, Part I."

I am an Ocean City seagull, and Ed wrote a poem about my activities at the beach at Ocean City, Maryland. I spotted Ed as he was walking a few days ago. I was really glad to see him. Ed told me he was going to write a sequel poem about me. We talked it over and decided there was too much information to put in a poem, so Ed decided to write a short story; a very short story about me.

I don't know if you're aware that a seagull has a year of life ratio similar to dogs and humans. One year of a dog's life is equal to approximately seven years. When it comes to seagulls, the ratio is twelve years. That would mean that I am around sixty years old. A lot has happened in the past sixty years, which would be five human years.

After Ed went home with his wife Janet, I decided to get a gull wife and raise a family. The beach life was taking a toll on my heart. I met a nice gull named Bertha. She was born and raised on the bay side of Ocean City. Her parents raised her on nothing but tuna. Myself, I spent the first year of my life on tourist hand-me-downs until I established a more permanent beach route.

Bertha and I had three child gulls: one male and two females. There names are Blinky Jr., who everyone calls BJ, Benita, and Beulah.

BJ graduated with honors from the Ocean City Scavenger Academy. He followed in my web prints and is well known on the local beaches. Benita eventually settled down and became a stay in the nest mom gull. Beulah is a different story. She was forever cutting classes and was eventually asked to leave the Seagull Wing Beautification business school. She ended up with the wrong school of gulls and started selling herself for peanuts. The other day I heard that she and a bunch of losers were flying down to Miami to slut around the beaches there. Hey, I'm too old to worry about her now.

I recently retired and Bertha and I moved to a rooftop condo on the west side of Ocean City.

The condo is located right next to a Chinese restaurant. They load the dumpster up with fish every night, so I don't have to cruise the beaches anymore. Life is grand for Bertha and I, but I'm awfully worried about Ed. He's actually writing a short story about me, a fictional seagull. I think he may have gone over the edge; too much writing, I imagine.

Well, I may write to you next summer if Ed comes back to Ocean City.

Later, Blinky

HENRI - A RESCUE

    Hi, my name is Henri, and I'm a rescue dog. I'm anywhere from four to six years old. Nobody seems to really know. They all say: "We think he's four to six years old," but believe me that I could be thirty for all anyone really knows. I'm part Beagle and part Bassett Hound and I look like a cute Beagle stretched out to the length of a Beagle Hound. My new step-parents are going to get something from Amazon that they send away for and when the results are sent back to them, my true identity will be known. Yeah, I bet ya!

    I've been to three or four foster homes so far, so I hope this one lasts. I'm tired of breaking all these people in, not to mention all the territory I have to mark again. My new step-parents look normal, but so did a couple of the other ones. She seems nice, but he seems a little crude, always passing gas and burping real loud, but I understand that most men are like that. They're both retired so they have all day, every day, to feed, pet, and suck up to me. I hope the people at the adoption agency told them that I won't stay in a crate. I already destroyed two of those suckers. I found out when I arrived here that I suffer from separation anxiety. I probably picked that up at the vet's office when they neutered me. What a day that was. When a dog gets that done, I think they should do it to the owners as well. There would be a lot less neutering going on in Tinsletown, folks.

    I think that separation thing started the other

day. They both left at the same time to eat at a Chinese Buffet restaurant. They were gone for two full hours. I scratched the shit out of the back door but I couldn't get out . I ripped the mini-blinds off the front window after I ripped the drapes off the rods. Boy, were they pissed! I thought the big guy was going to hit me. Lord knows I had enough of that. He mellowed pretty fast though. Boy, these humans forget easily.

I've been in their house for about ten days now. I thought I had them trained pretty well until they had to go to church. They normally go together, but since we have the "one person at all times in the house" rule, they have to go at different times. He goes Saturday night, and then he drops her off at the front of church, and the two of us go around to the huge parking lot with tons of concrete and grass, until the Mass is over. Thank God dogs aren't allowed in church. You should have heard the crap they were singing.

So we drive around to the rear of church and parked way in the corner. He reads the Sunday paper for a little, checks the lottery, and says, "Okay, Shithead, time for you to take a crapolla!" I hate it when he calls me shithead. It's so demeaning. After I sniff and lick every blade of grass, I finally drop my deposit. He says, "Good boy." The next time he is up in the can doing his thing, I'm going to howl like crazy at his door. That's the same as "Good boy", I think.

Now we're back in the car and he says to me, "Now it's my turn." I hope he doesn't think he's going to leave me alone in this portable home on wheels. He is! I might as well start barking now in case anybody passes this thing and wants to save me. Hey, I bet you I can jump up to the front seat from back here. Yep, no sweat. Let's see, gum, wintergreen mints, and a dog snack. Oh yea, he said if I was good while he was gone he would have a surprise for me when he got back. Well, I'll have a surprise for him when he gets back. He's gonna' love the mess I made on this seat. Not!

Oh Boy, here he comes. I don't think he should be allowed to say all those swear words at me. At least I didn't get smacked. Thank God he's one of those humans that doesn't believe in hitting animals, of which I am one of. Oops, I understand you're not supposed to ever end a sentence in a preposition. Hey, what do I know? I'm only a dog.

Well it's time to pick up the Misses. She gets in and he starts whining at her about me and threatens to take me back to the adoption agency. I can see her smiling out of the side of her face because she knows that he doesn't mean it, and in the short ten days they've known me they've grown to love me.

She then asks the Big Guy why he didn't take me with him when he had to do his thing. He said, "Geeze, I never thought of that." I've also heard, "The bigger they are, the dumber they are."

I would have liked to see the inside of a human's bathroom. Well it's time to go home and do some more human training on them. I hope they're up to it.

The Misses just made a list of places they wanted to go where that they couldn't take me. They decided they would have to hire a dog sitter. I hope it's somebody I can take advantage of.

Oops! There goes that preposition at the end of a sentence again.

It looks like I'm gonna' like it here – free food, lodging, and affection. I couldn't ask for more. I understand that they go to church every Sunday. Maybe I'll get to see a men's room.

Henri

HOLD ON, ALICE

Our house was at the bottom of a hill in Beechview, which – like many neighborhoods in Pittsburgh – had its share of very steep streets. I lived on at the bottom section of Belasco Street, which consisted of five or six blocks of hilly terrain. When we had at least 5 or 6 inches of snow, Belasco was impossible to travel on.

It was a bonanza for all the children when no cars could travel on Belasco due to snow though, because it became a prime location for sledding.

Our house, like most homes in the 1950s, was equipped with a coal furnace. I and other neighborhood kids had to retrieve ashes from our coal furnaces as a vital preparation for sledding. Belasco was such a very steep hill that ashes had to be spread at the bottom of the hill to slow down and stop the speeding sleds. If these ashes weren't spread you would face a twenty-five to thirty foot drop to another street below the hill. Nobody ever fell down to this other street, but I imagine if someone did they would be seriously hurt or even killed.

Occasionally, some of the fathers would participate in these sled riding parties. One of my friends, Joey Schratz, would always sled with us and his father would join every once in a while. I called Mr. Schratz as Mr. Schratz, but Mrs. Schratz was addressed as Alice. She told us she wanted to be one of the boys, so Alice it was.

One Friday night we were bored with just

riding down the hill individually. We decided to tie three sleds together and see what happened. The Schratz's home was at the top of the hill, right where we began our decent. After tying the sled together we were ready.

Just then, Mr. Schratz and Alice came running out of their house yelling, "Hold up, we want to go down with you guys." A couple of us talked it over and decided Mr. Schratz was OK, but we didn't want a girl going down the hill with us, especially a girl who was an old lady – Alice must have been at least 30 at the time.

We mentioned this to Mr. Schratz, who in turn must have told Alice. Alice told us that she used to sled ride all the time when she was younger. We talked it over again with Mr. Schratz and decided we would let Alice come along. Mr. Schratz would ride in the front sled, then me, then Joey, and then we got a little sled for Alice, which we tied to after the third sled.

We were ready. We started down the hill. Everyone was yelling, especially Alice, who was screaming bloody murder. As we approached the ashes we always held on because it was usually an abrupt stop. Everyone held on this time except Alice. I guess we failed to tell her about holding on to the sled when hitting the ashes.

When her sled did hit the ashes she went flying through the air, still screaming, but more intense now. She landed in a big, dead jagger bush, which slowed her decent. We all ran over to her. She had a few scratches on her face, but otherwise seemed to be okay.

Mr. Schratz was a somewhat quiet man

who never showed too much of a sense of humor. When he realized that Alice was just shaken up, he said to her, "Alice, I'm really a little mad at you."

She said, "Why, John?"

"I saw you flying through the air," he replied, "and you didn't even stop to say hello." That's the first time I had ever heard Alice swear. In fact, she swore at Mr. Schratz all the way up the hill.

That was the last time the Schratzs went sledding with us. At least I found out Mr. Schratz's name was John.

I know this seems like a lot of writing to get to the "Alice flying through the air" part, but it was an unforgettable night. I can still see her sailing over my head. It's like those commercials you see on TV – priceless, because it truly was.

SISTER IGNATIUS

This is a little story about Sister Ignatius, a Sister of St. Joseph nun who teaches English at St. Bonaventure School in the Pittsburgh area of Pennsylvania. The Sister has been a nun and educator for over fifty years.

Sister Ignatius has a nasty secret she would like to get out in the open, but she's afraid her past and current students would chastise her in the religious community. This secret has been going on for the past forty years and she almost told it to Sister Mary Bernard last year, but chickened out at the last minute. She was too embarrassed to admit it to anyone. This secret is not something that she would carry to the church confessional. I would say that it's morally objectionable, but it wouldn't be considered a sin in the eyes of the Catholic Church.

Sister's habit started around the time she entered high school. She didn't practice this nasty habit every day, but it soon blossomed into a regular happening. In the beginning it was once or twice, which grew into fifty or sixty times per day. She couldn't resist the urge to cheat at this word buffet. Sister knew that there are a lot of people in the world who do this, but she knew that it didn't make it right. The guilt had utterly consumed her and she had trouble sleeping at night.

You would think with her education Sister would not have reason to practice her habit, but, you see she was a crossword junkie and always looking for the answers in the back of the book.

Sister is currently under a doctor's care trying to cure herself of this devastating scar on her integrity. But between you and me, dear reader, I don't think she has a chance at rehabilitation, because I asked what her chances of a cure were and she said, "I wish I had a clue," – poor sister!

The Early Life and Adventures of Freddie

FREDDIE'S FIRST MASS

I wonder why they're getting me up so early this morning. I know today is Sunday and I'm pretty sure that the doctor's office is closed today. Mom's putting my new jean outfit on that Aunt Peggy bought me for my third birthday. It really must be some place special if I'm going to put on new clothes, and if I'm not mistaken Mom and Dad are wearing new clothes as well. For as long as I can remember Dad and I slept in on Sundays. Mom always went somewhere by herself. I think she was just taking a break from Dad. I wonder if I'm going to get something to eat before we leave this morning. Oh boy, here comes Mom with a bottle of milk. I guess I'll eat something when we all get back home.

Oh my God! I just had a scary thought. Maybe they're going to take me back to the hospital where they picked me up. Nah, I've been pretty good so far. There's no reason for them to take me back. Besides, they had to go through a lot of physical activity to conceive me.

Well, here we go. I've never been to this building before; it's huge. I'm glad I'm not asleep; those darn bells would surely have woken Dad and me up.

Boy, this place must be high-class—everyone is dressed to the nines. Oh wait, there's a few slobs dressed in jeans and sweatshirts; maybe they're poor. There sure are a lot of steps to get into this place. This baby carrier Dad bought is nice, but I'm on my back most of the time. I never get to see anything until he takes me out of here. Hey, I hear organ music. I hope they're not taking me to a funeral; I've heard they're very depressing.

Wow! Would you take a look at this ceiling? I betcha Leonardo DaVinci himself painted it.

We stopped moving. Maybe Dad will lift me out of this carrier so I can see where I am.

This is one huge hall. I can see a lot of my neighbors from my street, and there's that cute looking redhead that lives next door. I see she's still on the bottle. That's probably why she's so darn skinny, no solid food to beef her up. I wonder if they have any food in here. Maybe if I scream real loud somebody will bring me something. Man, I didn't know I could screech that loud. I betcha' that redhead was impressed. I don't think Mom was; she's taking me to the back of this place to a gigantic glass room. I feel like one of the contestants on the Family Feud.

I've been quiet for a few moments, so Mom is taking me back to where the action is.

Hey, I recognize that bald guy in the green cape over there. He's the one who almost drowned me a couple of years ago. I still can't figure out why my mom and Dad just stood there as he dropped my little head in that deep fountain.

I wonder where he bought that outfit anyway. I know they don't sell anything like that at Wal-Mart, but I bet in a few years they probably will. I hope that he doesn't try to put any oil on my forehead again. The last time he did some of it rolled in my eyes, and I couldn't see for a couple of days.

I'll tell you what; I wish they would make up their minds. I'm getting dizzy watching all these people getting up and down. Do they want to stand, kneel, or sit? Make up your mind, people!

What's this? There's a bunch of guys with baskets collecting money and envelopes. I hope they don't expect any money from me; I don't even have a job yet.

Now we're talking. That bald headed guy is standing up there passing out food. It looks like they are little white Frisbees. Hey, we're getting up to get our food. That guy gave Mom and Dad their food, but all I got was a pat on the head. I should feel happy; at least he didn't try to drown me again.

All those people in the corner are starting to sing. They're singing songs that I never heard on the radio or TV at home. I wonder if they take requests, I'm dying to hear Madonna's new song. What's going on now? Everyone is shaking hands and kissing each other. Maybe it's going to get a little risqué around here. No chance; everyone is starting to leave.

I can't believe my dad is shaking hands with that bald headed guy, after he tried to drown me. Oh my God! He kissed my mom on the cheek. I hope he's not going to be my new dad. If he is, I'm going to have to take some swimming lessons real quick. It doesn't hurt to be prepared. Though in this case it would probably save my life.

All in all this was a good learning experience for me. I'll tell you one thing though, if we're going to do this next week I'll make sure that my mom gives me some solid food before we go. I can't make a meal out of those little white Frisbees.

FREDDIE AT THE CAR WASH

Well, it looks like I'm going to share another adventure with my dad. I heard him tell Mom to sleep in because he was taking us someplace to get our car washed. I like going on trips with Dad because he lets me eat all kinds of food that mom says are not good for me. I don't know why she says that, because I like the food Dad gives me.

I know why Dad is taking our car to a wash place. My dad always washes the car when our neighbor, Miss Bunns, would wash hers. She always wore a bathing suit that was chopped in half when she washed her car and Dad would always help her until Mom would come outside. I always wondered why she never helped Dad wash Miss Bunns' car or why she never helped to wash ours. I guess she was always tired from doing cooking and cleaning stuff.

"Mr. Magic." Now that's a funny name for a place you get your car washed at. I guess there's a guy in this big building that waves some kind of wand and the car is magically washed. Hey, why are we staying in the car? There's a lot of water in this place and me and Dad didn't wear our swimming trunks. I didn't see a guy with a wand so I guess we just sit in here and the car gets washed. I know my dad knows what he's doing because he's a lot older and smarter than anyone I know.

My God, what's all that soapy water they're putting on our car? My dad will never be able to drive with that gunk on our windshield. Oh, wait a minute. Now they're putting clear water on the car to clean the soap off. I have to go number two. I sure did pick a bad week to be potty trained. I have to get to a toilet or I'll have to do cucky in my underwear. I never thought to take a pair of rubber pants with me. I wonder if Dad wears the rubber kind. I could borrow his.

I can see that crying isn't going to do me any good because Dad is screaming and they still won't let us out of this car. I think he may be claustrophobic or scared of tight places.

Well, we finally stopped moving, but it's too late. The magician guy told my dad that he could take me to the bathroom while some guys were going to clean our windows. I hope they spray some deodorant in our car; it sure does smell like crap in there!

FREDDIE GOES TO MARKET

I wonder why Mom is getting me up so early. I see the old man is still in bed. Oh, I forgot. It's Saturday and he doesn't go to work today. I don't blame him for staying in bed. The last time Mom dragged the two of us out of bed early, we went to that church. What a fiasco that was. Mom said to me, "We're going to let your father sleep in today. He doesn't like food shopping." Food shopping, what the heck is that? Hey, I'm game, another adventure.

Wow! This parking lot is bigger than the one when we went to church. I guess all the men sleep in on Saturdays. All I see in this parking lot is mothers with their kids.

Look at these neat huge chrome kid carriers. There's some over there that are big plastic cars. I guess I'm not old enough to drive one of those, and I think Mom is too big to get into one. Mom told me to pay attention at the way she shops. She says when she's too old to do this I can take over the job. I don't know where the heck Dad is going to be.

I thought that church was a big building but this one is humongous. Dad's always complaining about the light bill and reminds Mom to turn the lights out when she's not using them. He ought to see the lights here, and they're all turned on.

My God, I've never seen so many fruits and veggies in one spot. There must be a huge garden around here somewhere. I think Mom squeezed every fruit and vegetable before she put them in those child suffocating bags. There's a guy in a uniform standing in the corner. He may be a cop, but he doesn't have a gun. He just watched my mom and all these other people steal what they want. I don't know why Dad didn't come with us. He didn't have to worry about getting caught.

I've never seen so many cans in my life. It looks like someone grabbed the stuff from the fruit and veggie section, shrunk them up, and stuffed them in these different shaped cans. I think the cans may be heavier, but what do I know, I'm just a kid.

You know, I don't see anyone paying for the stuff they're grabbing. Hey, what does that guy want with my mom's purse? He probably needs money to buy some soap so he can take a bath. I don't know why he needs money. He can get anything he wants for free in this place. Where's my mom? Oh, there she is talking to that guy who looks like a cop, but doesn't carry a gun. I think I'll scream. Boy, that dirty guy can really move, and he forgot to take my mom's purse with him.

Well, things have quieted down a bit and Mom is back over there talking to that guy in the milk aisle. Too bad I have such a limited vocabulary—I'd tell Dad about that sleezeball who tried to steal Mom's purse. The guy must not be afraid of getting caught because he's wearing a shirt with his name on the back of it, Penn State.

Wow! Look at all the meat. All you have to do is take a little paper number, get that number called, point at the stuff you want, and they hand it to you. This place is great!

Now we're in the "frozen vegetable" aisle.

I don't get this place. When we first came in this place my mom picked out the veggies she wanted and put them in this chrome cart. Then she got the same thing that was shrunken up and squeezed in these little cans. Now, we get the same things that were taken out of the little cans and then frozen and stuffed in little cold bags. Let us make up our minds, people. I hope Dad knows what's going on here.

Hey, there's that girl that lives down from our house. I guess her mom is also a thief. She has a lot more stuff in her cart than we do. I wonder why she's smiling at me. She probably wants to have a relationship, but I'm not ready for that.

I guess it's okay if I leave a little stinker in this cart. Wow! That was a doozy. Maybe I should not have had those prunes for breakfast. I'll just point my finger at my mom, like I do at home. Dad always laughs, but nobody is laughing here.

"Check Out." Now there's a new word. It turns out we do have to pay for this stuff anyway. My faith has been renewed in my fellow man and especially my mom. Besides that, I'm way too young to be going to prison.

FREDDIE - OUT TO LUNCH

Mom has been in a good mood all morning. She keeps going around the house singing. Boy, I could do without that. I hope she doesn't sing in the church choir. Maybe this happiness has something to do with the phone call she got this morning from Aunt Sophie. I like my Aunt Sophie, but I think she is color blind. Some of the outfits she has bought me are downright hideous. I know when all my cousins and I get together, we look like a meeting of distasteful hand-me-down children who are unfortunately not responsible for the rags they wear.

I now know why Mom is so happy. We are going to pick up Aunt Sophie and go to some place called lunch, whatever that is. I'm ecstatic that Mom is driving. The last time Aunt Sophie drove, she scared the crap out of me, literally. Thank God Mom always carries extra diapers when Aunt Sophie drives. Aunt Sophie would give Evil Knievel a run for his money. I bet she got her driver's license through a correspondence course over that internet thing. I think I better start crying because it always works when I'm hungry. I cry and instantly I get strained tasteless food or a big bottle of lukewarm milk. I wonder what cold milk tastes like. All the grown-ups drink it that way.

Mom just said, "Don't cry Freddie, you'll get something to eat when we go to lunch with Aunt Sophie." At my age I learn something new every day. Today I learned that food and lunch must be the same thing.

Well, we're at Aunt Sophie's house and she's

waiting for us, and you won't believe the get-up she has on today. She must be buying her clothes at the same place she's buying the outrageous rags she buys for me. I sure hope we're not in a car accident. The less people that see her, the better off the world will be. I can't believe that she would come out of the house looking like that. Now here she comes to give me one of her overly sloppy kisses. Mom has to wipe my face off with my blanket after one of those sloppers. I know Aunt Sophie means well, but give me a break.

We've stopped at a parking lot, so this must be the lunch food place. Mom let Aunt Sophie carry me in to this place while she tried to park our car. Aunt Sophie is not the most coordinated person in the world. I hope she doesn't drop me.

Wow, there sure are a lot of people in this place. They must not have any food at home or they wouldn't be in this place to get some lunch food. It's funny though, I don't hear anyone crying because they want to eat. There are a lot of people in here who look like they don't have to eat anymore. I'd say the majority of these folks are at least a 2XL, and there maybe even a few 5 and 6XLs. Oh God, here comes someone else who is going to pinch my face. I'll use my inner defense mechanism. I'll throw up. They always seem to back off when I do that.

Mom and Aunt Sophia are looking at these paper things called menus. They list all the food that this place must cook for people. I hope they can cook me up something better than that crappy strained so-called gourmet baby food Mom tries to shove down my throat. Mom and Aunt Sophia ordered something called hamburgers. I'm no dietician but all the crap they ordered to go on those hamburgers will surely put their cholesterol at the danger level. I don't think those onion rings are going to help their total either. Mom ordered chicken broth for me, but she failed to ask me how I wanted it done, rare, medium, or well done. I can see I'm not going to get any fatter in this place.

Mom's going to one of those toilet places like they have at the grocery store. I hope Aunt Sophie can handle me by herself for a couple of minutes. I hope she doesn't try to pick me up with all that hamburger grease on her hands. I may slip out of her hands and right out onto the floor. Oh God, she is going to kiss me again. Instant sloppy. Whoa, does she have some nasty breath. It's probably those greasy onion rings. I hope Mom has some of that Scope in her purse because I'm gonna' need it. Hey, what's she doing now? Doesn't she know I'm not allowed to eat whole foods? I'm liable to choke to death. Hey, this hamburger stuff is pretty good. I hope she doesn't try to shove any onion rings down my throat. Oh God, here comes the rings, and here comes Mom screaming. I didn't know that sisters screamed at each other like that. I'm glad I don't have one, but if I did I'd never scream at her. Mom sure is setting a bad example for me, although I could have choked to death on the stuff that Aunt Sophie was trying to shove down my throat.

Now they're ordering something called pies. I think I have eaten one of these, but you can never tell when they grind it up to the consistency of mud. Hey, they look pretty good. I don't know why the other people in this place don't eat pie instead of eating hamburgers and onion rings first.

Now they're arguing who is going to take care of the check, whatever that is. All I know is that I want to get out of here before another lady comes over and flashes me a smile and tells my mom how cute I am. Hey, they don't have to tell her. We all know how cute I am.

This has been another learning experience for me. I'd like to go back there again, but only when I'm old enough to eat pie. Oh, and I don't want to go with Aunt Sophie. That woman is dangerous!

FREDDIE TAKES IN A BASEBALL GAME

Time for another new adventure. It's called a baseball game. I heard Dad tell Mom we were going to go there today. Mom thought I was too young, but Dad said that you're never too young to go to a baseball game. Whatever that is.

I wonder why Mom and Dad are wearing those strange hats. They even have one for me. Boy is this sucker ever tiny!

I can't believe the traffic today. There must be something better to do on a Sunday afternoon. Hey, most of the people in this traffic are wearing the same silly hats as Mom and Dad and me. Some even have shirts the same colors as their hats. Wow, look at the size of this parking lot. Twenty bucks to park. Now that's just plain crazy. I'm just a kid and I know that's out of control. I see why it's twenty bucks to park. Everyone gets to sit around and tell funny stories and drink free beer.

Boy is this place huge. The sign out front said, "Yankee Stadium." Thirty bucks admission. Are they nuts? Thank God we don't go here every day. Otherwise Mom would have to get a part-time job to pay for it all. At least we saved a few dollars on me. I think because it's my first time here they let me in for free. I thought the church had a lot of people in it, and then the food store had more, but this place has got to take the cake. There must be a couple thousand people here, or more.

I can't believe my dad paid thirty bucks for

these seats. If we got any higher up, I think we could probably touch Heaven. I'm surprised everyone up here doesn't have a nose bleed, because I think I'm ready to have one. I don't see any oxygen stations up here, but they sure could use them.

Hey, there's some guy selling that funny food on funny bread. I think Dad called them "hot dogs." I know I'm not getting any of those. I saw Mom packing some stewed carrots in my tote bag. Sure, I eat stewed carrots and they gorge themselves on hot dogs. Seems fair.

Everybody is standing up and screaming. I wonder what happened? There's a bunch of guys running out on a green field, and they're throwing a little white ball back and forth to each other and catching it in these big fat brown gloves. Now there's a guy standing in front of this white thing on the ground holding a big stick in his hands. It looks like he's trying to hit the white ball this other guy is throwing at him. If the other guy got a lot closer I think the guy would have a better chance of hitting the ball. There are four or five guys standing around dressed in black suits wearing Darth Vader masks. I saw Darth Vader in a movie once. It looks to me like if a guy spits something out he has stored in his jaw the guy in black tells him to sit down. Sometimes the guy standing in front of the white thing hits the little white ball and runs like the devil. When he hits the ball, everyone stands up and screams. Come to think of it, I've seen this kind of activity being done in the street in front of our house, but they're all little kids, not big guys like I'm seeing today. This thing they're doing looks pretty boring to me. I think I'd rather be home watching paint dry. Maybe if I throw up Mom and Dad will take me home. I can't believe that Dad spends all of that money to see a bunch of guys run around like a bunch of kids. If Dad really wanted to see this kind of thing he just has to sit on the front porch and watch it some days. And it would be free then, too.

Now we're all standing up to sing. I never heard this song on the radio or TV: "Take me out to the ballgame." Hey, that's where we must be: at a ballgame. When I grow up, I sure the heck am not going to put my kid through this. What a rip!

Hey, there's my next store neighbor, Mr. Johnson. I heard Dad say he may be getting laid off from his job. I wonder what "laid off" means? I see he got another job anyway. He wipes off peoples seats before they sit in them, and then most of them hand him a dollar. It looks like a really cool job, but he has to watch these guys playing games all day.

Thank God we're leaving. I hope we don't land in a giant traffic jam like we did when we came here. My plastic underwear will only hold so much, and then it's like Armageddon.

Dad told Mom he had a good time. I'm glad somebody did. He says he can't wait for football season because he can take me to one of those games. He said he knew since I had such a good time at the baseball game that I would enjoy football even more. I wonder which kid he was with today. I don't even think Mom enjoyed that fiasco today. She just acted like she liked it to please my dad.

Well, it's time to watch a little television. What's on the menu, Dad? Crap. He turned on a baseball game!

FREDDIE VISITS
A NEIGHBOR

Boy, I had a rough night last night. I think I'll just sleep all day. I think Mom and Dad might have had one as well because I kept hearing all these weird moans and groans coming from their room. No wonder I didn't get any sleep. I hear Mom coming now. Boy is she in a good mood. I wonder how she can be so happy when she didn't get her eight hours of shut-eye.

Mom told me that she sent Dad to work and we are going to visit our next door neighbor, Miss Vicky. I think she's the hot looking blond who's always smiling at my dad, except when Mom's around. Miss Vicky must be poor, otherwise why would Mom be taking all these desserts over for her. I heard Dad say that Miss Vicky's guy had a great job working at a laundry. Dad said that he launders more money than anyone he knows. He must make more than my dad because his house is bigger, their car is bigger, and they have a pool in their back yard. Dad says that "Vicky has one in the oven." I have no idea what that means but I'll be sure to check their ovens when I go over there.

Wow, this place is huge. The living room is bigger than our whole downstairs. I don't know why we're bringing cake to her; with that huge belly it looks like she's been eating a lot of cake, and pie, and ice cream.

Look at the size of that TV— it almost takes up the whole freakin' wall! I bet you ister and Miss

Vicky watch a lot of body education movies on that thing. It probably gives you a nice bird's eye view of the good parts of the anatomy. I'm just saying, ya know?

What a huge kitchen. There are more appliances in here than that Sears store we visited last week. I checked both the microwave and the big super oven and there's nothing in them. I don't know what Dad was talking about when he said there was one in the oven. If there was something in there, she must have taken it out before we got there. Thank God Mom brought my milk. It looks like Miss Vicky is going to serve that hot brown water that most grown-ups drink. Ugh!

Well, time for the customary house tour. This house is so big we may have to take a couple of sandwiches with us since we'll be gone so long. I can't believe it – five bedrooms – and they all look the same except for one humongous one. Miss Vicky sure did get embarrassed when that box with the whips and chains fell out of her cupboard. I thought that maybe she works part-time at the local circus.

Ah, a visit to the pool. This baby is so big I wouldn't be surprised if the U.S. team practiced here for the upcoming Olympics. Boy, Miss Vicky even has her own lifeguard. She introduced him to my mom – his name is Julio, and if I was a female, I think I'd take a shot at him. The way Miss Vicky is eye-balling him, I think she has.

Miss Vicky told my mom that her man was going to be out of town for about a week. She asked my mom if my dad could come over and repair a few things for her. My mom told her that my dad was really busy doing things at our house. I don't know why my mom lied to Miss Vicky. All my dad does at home is lie on his recliner, watch TV, and drink beer. Maybe Mom doesn't want Dad to see how big Miss Vicky's house is.

FREDDIE'S FIRST YARD SALE

Boy, Mom sure is excited today. She's been running around for a couple of hours now. I don't even think she even had her first cup of coffee yet. It's a Saturday and Dad usually sleeps in because he doesn't have to go to work, but he was up before Mom today. I wonder what's going on.

It looks like Dad is getting ready to leave, and it doesn't look like I'm going with him, otherwise someone would be dressing me. Dad doesn't look real happy for a guy who has the day off.

He's talking to Mom now, and she doesn't look too happy either. He told her, "I did all the crap you wanted done in the front yard—you're on your own now. Don't worry about my dinner...I'll eat at a fast food joint and don't expect me until around six or seven. I don't know what I'm going to do all day—just as long as I'm not doing it here."

He gave her a big kiss and waved good-bye to me. I wonder if I'll ever see him again. I think the answer lies with the "crap in the front yard."

Mom told me that she would be busy all day and that my Aunt Sophie would be over to watch me. Oh boy, the queen of the sloppy kisses is coming over—I can't wait. Whatever Mom is doing today must be important because Aunt Sophie never shuts up, and Mom says she's a big gossip, whatever that is. Oh wow, I think she's at the door now.

Here comes the first sloppy kiss of the

day. At least I was prepared and knew she was coming. When you get down to it, being prepared doesn't mean anything. A sloppy kiss is a sloppy kiss. Aunt Sophie told me I was going to take a morning nap while she and Mom cook for all the people coming today. First of all, I just got up, and secondly, I still don't know why a bunch of people are coming to our house. I'll humor Aunt Sophie and lie down for a little while—I could use some beauty sleep.

I guess I was tired; I slept for almost an hour. Boy, it sure does smell good in here, but where is the food. We got smell, but no food. Here comes Miss Sloppy Kiss with a little sweater for me. I guess that means I'm going outside. Grown-ups walk around in short-sleeves, but they always put a sweater on the baby—I'm roasting my guts half the time.

What is all this junk doing in our front yard? Wait until Dad sees this. Wait a minute—I think that's what he was putting out on the lawn this morning. That big yellow sign says, "Yard Sale, make me an offer!" I'm not really that much into the monetary system yet, but by the looks of this crap, two bucks would be a fair price for everything.

It's nice of Aunt Sophie to give me the grand tour. The more I look at this stuff, the more I think it should be pushed to the curb for Saturday's junk pick-up, because that's what it is: junk! Here comes our neighbor Mr. Bronson, the infamous whistler. I don't think he'll take a chance at whistling at Mom while Aunt Sophie is here. If he did, I know Aunt Sophie would beat the snot out of him.

For Mom's sake I hope it doesn't rain. Joe,

the weather man said there was zero chance of precipitation (I guess that's rain) today, but I wouldn't count on it. The last time he was right, I wasn't even born yet.

I can't believe people are paying money for this junk. Mom has a lot of cash in that cigar box. Maybe if she gets enough money, she'll send Aunt Sophie to Mickey D's for some French fries. I need a break from Aunt Sophie anyway—she's starting to get on my last nerve.

It looks like the crowd has settled down. It's hard to believe that there's not much stuff left. I just can't figure people out—they'll buy anything as long as they think it's a bargain. I guess you could call Mom's yard sale a success, even though the yard is still here—nobody bought it.

Hey, Dad's home, and he's got a bag from Mickey D's with him. Good ol' Dad with some french fries for Freddie.

I hope I'm around to witness another one of these sales, but then I'll pick out the stuff we're gonna' sell!

FREDDIE GOES TO A PUBLIC SWIMMING POOL

Aunt Sophie is coming today to babysit Rose. Mom says she was really excited because she said she is much happier watching a girl than a boy. That doesn't say much for me and it's another black mark beside her name. If she's still alive by the time I grow up she will probably be way ahead of everybody as far as those black marks go, at the rate she's going now. I don't know if Rose is old enough to realize what a buffoon she is. Hey, what's wrong with me? This was supposed to be about swimming in a public pool, not Aunt Sophie. I shouldn't be talking about my dad's sister like that, but my mom does it all the time.

Okay, let's get back to the pool. The temperature today is supposed to reach 100 degrees. Mom decided we would go to Miss Vicky's for the afternoon because she has such a big pool. It appears that Miss Vicky's man friend came home early from his laundry job and caught Miss Vicky and Julio cleaning the pool together. Miss Vicky knows that Julio is the only one allowed to clean the pool. I don't know why she was helping Julio. Miss Vicky's man friend was mad and he poured a gallon of blue paint in the pool, so we, of course, can't go swimming there. Mom says that Miss Vicky had to let Julio go. I don't know what he was hanging on to.

Mom says that we would have to lower

ourselves and go to a public pool. I don't know what the difference is between a public pool and Miss Vicky's, but I'm sure I'm going to find out.

One difference is the size. This baby is as big as a football field. Boy, you can tell I'm aging; two weeks ago I didn't even know what a football was, more or less a football field. Ten bucks admission for Mom, and it's free for me; now that's a deal.

We put our bathing suits on under our civilian clothes so we wouldn't have to change with the commoners, Mom said, but we still had to take a shower with them. I wonder why Mom had to take another shower. She took one before we left home, and she gave me a horse bath. I think we watered up again because the water is blue like Miss Vicky's. Nope, wrong again. Mom says the water is clear but the pool is painted blue, creating an optical illusion. I'm not touching that one!

I wonder why we have to look like semi-nudists when we swim here. My dad told me what a nudist was last week. When we were watching Miss Vicky swim with no clothes on, Dad says that she was a nudist. Mom has a top and a bottom and I'm wearing a bottom, so that's why we're semi-nudists. Boy, I'm starting to pick up on this grown-up crap pretty fast.

Hey, where in the hell are we supposed to lie down? There must be a million people out here. Some of the girls would be arrested for public nudity if they dressed the way they are now out in the real world. Nobody cares how us boys look, or what we're not wearing.

Mom found a spot next to these old people.

"This will be okay. They don't look real friendly." Yeah, like we are.

Here we go; they have a special section just for little guys like me. There's a lot of moms in here as well. I guess they're afraid of the deep water. Hey, what's all that screaming over there? Some young stud with huge muscles is dragging some old lady out of the pool. Maybe she spit water on someone. Hey, he's starting to kiss her. You know, I believe in free enterprise, but I think this stud could do a lot better than that over-the-hill mama. What's he doing now? It looks like he's trying to crush her chest. It must be some new kind of sexual move I haven't seen Mom and Dad do.

Mom said she thought we had enough excitement for one day and that we better start heading home. Mom thought it was an exciting day because of the people she saw having sex outside of the pool. Mom did say that these people were different; I can only imagine what was going on inside the pool.

We had to stop at a restaurant and get Aunt Sophie a hamburger and onion rings. I'll be sure to get one of her sloppy kisses before she eats the onion rings, and then I'll make myself scarce when it's time for her to leave. I better check on Rose. After all, she was with this madwoman most of the afternoon. Well, Rose looks okay, but I do see a few wrinkles that weren't there when we left our home.

I heard the guy on the TV say it was going to be 100 degrees again today. It's a shame I don't have any religion yet, otherwise I'd be praying for rain, and lots of it.

FREDDIE'S FIRST VISIT TO A JAPANESE BUFFET... YUM YUM

Boy, Mom and Dad are sure in a good mood today. Dad has been going around the house smiling and whistling. I know he's not happy because it's Saturday, because on Saturdays he always works in the yard, and that usually depresses him. And Mom is all giggly; she told me she didn't have to cook dinner today, and I think that made Dad happy because I think he thinks Mom is not a good cook. Boy, there were sure a lot of "thinks" in that last sentence. What do you think? I think I got my mom's sense of humor, because I know I sure didn't get it from my dad.

I wonder why Mom tried to starve herself and Dad today; she included me in that. How could she do that? I'm still a growing boy in his formative years, whatever that means. Well wherever we're going, it must not be fancy—everyone is wearing their scrappy clothes.

When Mom got in the car she said to Dad, "I'm starving, I can't wait to eat. Aunt Sophie said this place was good. If anyone knows about a buffet she does."

Dad said, "It better be good. I was almost ready to start eating today's newspaper." He added, "I think it will be a good eating experience for Freddie. He's never been to a buffet and I think it may help prepare him for the real world."

I think the lack of food has affected Dad's mind because he's not making a lot of sense. How could almost starving me to death and then taking me to a buffet prepare me for the real world? I'd rather eat at my normal times and worry about the world later.

I just had a scary thought. I heard Mom mention Aunt Sophie's name... I hope to God she's not at this buffet thing we're going to. I'm already starving, but seeing her usually makes me lose my appetite.

Dad's pulling in to a huge parking lot. The big sign on the building reads, "Jin's Japanese Restaurant: The Largest Buffet in North America." Boy, this guy Jin is really on an ego trip, "The Largest Buffet in North America." I bet if I knew how to drive a car I could find a bigger one.

Boy, I never saw so much food displayed at one time. I can't believe how many different ways they sell chicken here. There simply has to be a chicken coop out back somewhere. Oh, and some rice patties. There's a lot of that stuff here too.

I've never seen so many short black-haired people in my short life. I've got some news for the little black-haired girl who asked Mom if she wanted a booster seat for me—I'll probably be taller than her in a couple of years.

It appears you go get your own food in this restaurant. Dad didn't waste any time; the poor guy is starving. Like I'm not. Oh no, Mom is leaving me alone to fend for myself. Oh, never mind, she's just swiping some extra napkins from the table next to us. For a second there I thought I was all alone, like that poor little kid in the movie on the television. If the people who work in this restaurant thought I was all alone, they may take me in the back and color my hair black, so I'll look like them. They'll pick me because I'm smaller than them, not real big like Mom and Dad.

I'm really getting hungry. Maybe if I start crying they'll feed me. It works at home. I know Dad will lay a couple pieces of that chicken on me; he sure has enough on his plate.

Ah, here comes Mom with grub. Sure does look like a lot of chicken here. I hate to repeat myself, but I've never seen so many ways to cook chicken, if it really is chicken. I understand there's a lot of nasty rumors going around that these restaurants substitute their chicken for something else—Oh, the humanity!

Hey, Mom's giving me the grand tour. I noticed some pretty colored food, and she noticed me noticing it. She said, "Sorry Freddie, you wouldn't like that, it's all made out of raw fish."

I thought to myself, "If this stuff is raw, what the heck is it doing on display—somebody better pick it all up and take it back to the kitchen and cook it. It doesn't really bother me though. I don't think I like fish yet."

Well I guess we're all done eating. We made pigs of ourselves, and those extra napkins really came in handy. Hey, why is Mom putting some chicken in her purse? Maybe it's a midnight snack for Dad, and why is our waitress screaming at my mom? Oh, it appears that you can't take any of their food out of the restaurant. What a stupid rule that is, especially when it's out on display for anyone to take. Here comes an old guy with black hair—I can't believe he still has black hair; he has to be about 200 years old. He told Mom and Dad that our meal would be "no charge" for today. Wow, that's a good deal for us. He also told Mom and Dad that we were banished from his restaurant for the rest of our lives. I know Mom and Dad don't have that long to live, because they're already really old, but I'm on my way up the ladder of life. This really sucks!

I don't believe my whole family has been banned from the largest Japanese restaurant in the world. How are we going to face the neighbors? Maybe we'll have to move. I really liked all of that chicken. If we move I'm sure there must be another one of those restaurants around—only smaller, of course.

Well except for all the chicken I ate, it turned out to be a really crappy day. And wait until you hear this folks, Mom was pilfering that chicken for Aunt Sophie. The woman wasn't even with us, and she gave me a headache. Wait until Aunt Sophie finds out it was her fault that we're banned from the largest buffet in North America. I wonder if Mom and Dad will consider disowning her. Nah, probably not.

FREDDIE'S FIRST TRIP TO THE LIBRARY... SHHHHH!

Well, another day, another adventure. We must not be going to a place that's real snazzy, because Mom is wearing her mid-life red jeans. The top she's wearing is so sheer you can almost see her bubbies through it, and she has on her patent leather boots. Boots and it's almost the middle of June. Boots! I do remember Mom telling Dad that the women today can wear almost anything they want, and at any time. Boy, he ought to see the way she is dressed today. I bet she'll come up with another theory for wearing those flashy red jeans and the patent leather boots.

Hey, she's putting scrubs on me now. Has she no pride dressing me up to look like an orphan? Oh God, she's getting rid of me! Nah, I'm too stinking cute to not keep around. Come on Mom, where are we going? She's got that smile like she's gonna' tell me something good.

Here it comes. She says, "I want you to be on your best behavior today, Freddie."

So much for hearing something good. Anyway, what's she talking about, "Behave myself?" I'm the closest thing to a saint as Mother Theresa, if she ever gets in, that is.

Mom told me if I'm good and don't make a lot of noise, she'll take me to a restaurant and buy me some French fries. I hope they're not the greasy ones like they sell at Mickey D's. The last time I ate the fries from there I got a severe case of kakadells. One day I heard Mom say that Kakadells meant you had a bad case of the runs. I've had them a few times and I sure don't want to go through that again.

Well, we're finally on the road. I don't know where we're going, but I can't wait to get home to tell Dad that Mr. Bronson, our neighbor, whistled at Mom. Mom always said that he was a dirty old man. Every time I've seen him, he looked pretty clean. Go figure. I just knew those red jeans were a mistake.

Here we are finally. This building must be a historic landmark. I've never seen one this old. Of course, when you get down to it, how many buildings have I saw? I always get that see, seen, saw thing screwed up. I think the right word should have been seen. Oh well, too bad. I'm learning as I go, people.

Boy, the inside of this building looks as old as the outside. Hey, there aren't any little people like me here, only old turds like Mom and Dad. I'll tell you one thing, every time I make a sound, someone looks at me and says, "Shhhh." It must be some kind of code word from a secret society, because everybody here says it.

Wow, look at all the books in here. I hope Mom doesn't think she's gonna' read all of them today. Because if she does, I'm gonna' hitch a ride home. I've never seen (I think I got it right this time) this many books in one place at one time. Dad keeps a lot of Playboy books under the bed, but not near as many as this place probably has.

That's the third "Shhhh" in the last ten

minutes. What do these morons expect me to do, go to sleep? I'm not that tired yet. Besides, I don't want to miss anything. Maybe some other guy will whistle at Mom and I can report that to Dad too. I think the new word is, "As well," instead of "Too." Ah, who cares. You know what I mean!

I'm really tired of doing nothing. I don't know how to read yet, otherwise I'd join all these perverts that are doing it. I don't know what pervert means, but maybe when I grow up it will probably be explained to me in one of these books.

Hey, I think we're leaving. Mom gave a card to the lady behind the big desk and then the lady punched a hole in it. That punch is probably for a greasy free order of fries when we get to Mickey D's. At least it didn't cost us any money to come here like the grocery store or the baseball stadium.

It'll be good to get home after a very boring day. I can't wait until Dad gets home so I can tell him about Mr. Bronson and the soon to be infamous whistle. I don't think Mom can wait till Dad gets home either because she got out of those red jeans mighty quick. I'm pretty sure I may witness my first fight between Mom and Dad tonight. I'll save the details of this fight for my next little story, if it happens. I think I'll call it, "Freddie witnesses his parent's first fight." What else would I call it?

FREDDIE WITNESSES HIS PARENT'S FIRST FIGHT

I just heard my mom talking on the phone to my dad. From what I gather from their conversation, there may be some excitement when he gets home. I can't believe she told Dad that she wore those red tight jeans and those high patent leather boots today when Mr. Bronson whistled at her. What was she thinking? I understand it's good to be truthful in your marriage, but I think she's being a little too truthful. I can't believe all the excitement over those jeans and boots. If I remember right, Dad bought the jeans last year for Mom's birthday.

I'm sure that Dad will be stopping to see Mr. Bronson before he comes home. I think he can whoop him; he probably only weighs 98 pounds and Dad is an almost fat 300. I wish I could see the skirmish, but Mom doesn't let me witness anything violent. I wonder what he's gonna' say to Mom. I bet ya' he's really pissed.

Hey, I hear Dad and Mr. Bronson laughing in front of Mr. Bronson's house. Why the heck are they laughing? They haven't even started fighting yet. I bet ya' Dad offered Mr. Bronson money to wimp out. I understand it's always a good idea to stay friends with your neighbors—you never know when you'll need them. Of course if someone broke into our house and we needed help, I don't think puny Mr. Bronson would be the one to call.

Here comes Dad, and he has a bag in his hands. It's probably dinner for tonight because he thinks after him and Mom fight, she won't be cooking. I hope he brought something to eat for me, maybe some more french fries.

Well the jig is up—it's show time! Dad walked through the door and plants a whopper of a kiss on Mom. What's going on here? I thought they were going to go round and round.

There was no food in the bag. Guess what? It was another pair of red jeans. Hey, I must be dreaming this stuff up, but I don't think so. It doesn't look like Mom and Dad are going to fight, but this stuff is off the page.

Dad told Mom to sit down on the couch, because he had something to say to her. Oh now, maybe the big guy is flooping the coop, or however they say that.

Dad looked at Mom. "I bought you another pair of red jeans for when the other pair I bought you wear out. After I thought about it, I like the fact that someone is still whistling at my wife. It means I made the right choice when I married you, and it also means that you still have it. And it means I might still have it, or I hope I do." There goes another of those big sloppy kisses.

Now Mom is crying. What for? It looks to me like she should be happy. Boy, I'll tell ya, in all my years, I'll never figure grown-ups out. Trying to figure them out will drive a person bonkers.

Dad says, "This calls for a celebration, I'm gonna' take my two favorite people out for something to eat. Where do you want to go, Sue?"

I'm thinking, I don't care where Mom wants to eat as long as they have good french fries.

Ah, another ending to a great day.

FREDDIE TAKES IN A PRO FOOTBALL GAME

It looks like we're all gonna' get dressed up again for something. Dad's excited because we're going to see his Jets. I thought Jets were a big plane that flew fast. We must have more cash than I thought if we own jets.

Mom filled me in that the Jets are a football team, whatever football is. She told me that football is similar to baseball, but they play with an odd shaped brown ball instead of a round white one. She also said that it's played on a different field than baseball and the players wear helmets instead of hats. She also added that in baseball, most of the players are usually skinny and run fast. But in football, most of the players are big and fat and try to beat the crap out of each other.

Similar my doopa! These games aren't at all alike. The only thing I think that's similar is they both have ball in their name. If I had my choice of games I think I'd like to play football. I think that I'd really enjoy beating the crap out of somebody and I think it may make me seem manlier than the little shit I actually am.

I see the same bandits are working these parking lots that were working the one for the baseball game. The only difference is 10 bucks. I guess they need the extra money to pay for insurance for beating up each other. I thought our seats were up high for the baseball game, but these babies are so far up I think I can probably talk to the guy who had something to do with making me.

I thought Mom and Dad were dressed a little crazy, but some of these idiots actually have paint on their faces. The people here seem a lot more radical than at the baseball game, and a lot drunker too. The slob in front of us has been drinking so much he won't remember who won the game.

Eight dollars for a small plastic bottle of beer. For the price of two more we could have brought a case with us. Seven dollars for a hot dog. I remember the ones from our visit to the baseball game. I'm pretty sure we could buy a whole freakin' cow for seven dollars. Now I know why Mom snuck cheese sandwiches in her purse. I heard some guy say they had some good roast beef sandwiches here. I guess it makes sense that they have ATM machines scattered all around. They're here so people can draw money out of them to help pay for the roast beef sandwiches.

Well it's about time the game started. Mom was right. These guys do beat the crap out of each other. If it wasn't for those guys in the prison uniforms giving the players a break every once in a while, I think most of them would probably kill each other. I think it's very nice of our government to give our inmates a part-time job on Sundays.

Everyone is screaming, "Touchdown! Touchdown!" I must have missed it when they screamed, "Throw-up! Throw-up!" because a couple of guys next to us are doing that right now. My mom always cleans up my throw-up. Maybe she can take care of these guys.

I'm getting tired of seeing all these guys running up and down that field. I'd take a nap but people won't stop screaming. Maybe if I start screaming Mom and Dad will take me home.

Fat chance – they can't even hear me. Somebody said it was half time and time to go take a leak. I've been leaking ever since we got here. In fact it's getting kind if moist down there. Maybe Dad will take me when he goes to leave his leak. Bingo – Dad told Mom he was going to go change me.

Boy does this place smell like pee. I think they should call it a pee station instead of a men's room. I've never heard so many grown men sigh in my life. They sound like they're happy to be here, despite the smell.

Okay – all dried up and ready to go back and see some big guys kick some butt.

Hey, where did they get that puny guy? If one of those big guys even passes gas they'll probably kill him. It looks like he's going to kick the brown ball. Dad says he's a very good field goal kicker. What the heck is a field goal kicker? Whatever it is must be pretty safe, because right after he kicked that ball, the other players turned around and ran the other way. I'll tell you what, this game looks a lot more complicated than baseball seemed.

Well, everybody is standing up, so it must be time to go. I hope Dad doesn't want to stop and see a baseball game – I don't think my little heart could take any more excitement. *Hic*

FREDDIE'S FIRST VISIT TO SANTA

Looks like Mom and I are going on another adventure. I haven't worn these dress-up clothes since we went to that place to see Uncle George. I can't believe all the people there crying, but all Uncle George did was sleep in that big puffy bed. Well, I got waylaid there a little. Now, back to my new adventure.

I wonder why I have to wear this red and white hat with my dressy clothes. It doesn't even match my outfit. I hate it when my stuff doesn't match! I saw a fat guy on TV wearing one of these red and white hats, but he also had on a matching red and white suit. At least he was matching.

Wow, this is a huge store and bigger than the market or the car wash we visited, but it isn't as big as the place they play baseball or football at. Wow, what the heck are these? I never saw stairs that move. Mom better hold on to me tight. This modern technology sure is scary. What will they think of next? Floors that move up and down?

Boy, there sure are a lot of toys on this floor. If I would have known we were going to pick up toys, we could have rented one of those "U-hauls." Mom probably can't handle one of those. She can barely drive a small car. Wow, look at the length of this line. There must be a hundred kids here with their moms or dads. There are even kids here by themselves. I heard one guy tell his wife that he was going to go get lit up. I guess he was gonna' put lights on himself like our Christmas tree.

I wonder what the big attraction is. Hey, I can make out something now. It's a guy in one of those red and white suits like I saw on that guy on TV. There were a couple more dressed like that on the street corners too. They all had big white beards that were there to probably cover up some pimples or something else defective on their faces. I can't believe there are that many old fat guys walking around with bad complexions.

It looks like the moms are putting the smaller kids like me on the big guy's lap. I don't know what I'm going to do when Mom puts me on his lap. I'm not supposed to talk to strangers. Hey wait, I don't even talk yet. I guess I'll just make those gibberish sounds like I always do and let everybody say how cute I am.

Well here goes. Boy this guy has nasty breath! It smells like that bald guy in the church we visit. This guy's teeth are yellow, which aren't a good match for that white beard. Mom told him a bunch of stuff I wanted for Christmas, whatever that is. I didn't even know I wanted that stuff. She also asked this Santa guy for a baby sister for me. She didn't ask me or Dad about that. Mom said that Santa will be at our house on Christmas Eve to drop off presents for me. If he brings a sister for me, I hope she's not crying because I need my beauty sleep.

Mom said that Santa will give me a gift from his bag today. He reached in and grabbed a little toy pistol wrapped in plastic. Doesn't he know about guns for kids, the dangers of swallowing a small toy, and suffocating on plastic toy wrappers? I've seen better toys in cereal boxes, to be honest, and they looked a lot safer too. I hope this isn't a preview of the toys I'm getting on Christmas Eve.

Mom said that we'll be coming back next year; I can't wait. Now we're on our way to Eat 'N Park for lunch and we're supposed to meet Aunt Sophia there. If she gives me one of those sloppy kisses again, I'm going to poop my pants before she can get me to that place where they change my diapers. That'll fix her.

Well, another day in the life of "Freddie, the super baby."

FREDDIE GETS A SISTER

It sure is busy around here this morning. Mom and Dad have Aunt Sophie coming over to baby sit me. Oh, I hear her at the door now. Oh my, she's still dressing like an old frump. I think she needs a man. Then maybe she'll take care of herself a little better. I hope nobody saw her coming in our house. Oh boy, here she comes with her first sloppy kiss of the day. I hope she brought extra napkins. Aunt Sophie told me that my mom and dad were going to the hospital and that's why she is here to watch me. I sure hope Dad is taking Mom to get that giant basketball taken out of her tummy. Dad said that was another game we still had to see and that they played this game indoors.

Mom does all of those exercises in front of the TV every day. I thought she did those to lose weight, not get a bigger belly. Boy, I'll never figure grown-ups out.

Aunt Sophie told me that Mom was going to bring me home a present from the hospital. I hope it's not Mom's basketball. I don't even know how to play that game yet.

Hey! Dad's home, but where is Mom? And, I don't see any basketball. Dad told me that Mom was going to stay at the hospital for a couple of more days. He said that he had to work during the day so Aunt Sophie would watch me until Mom comes home. I don't know if I can take a couple of more days of Aunt Sophie. That woman really drives me up a wall.

Well this is the third day. I hope Dad keeps his promise and tells Aunt Sophie to go home.

Here he comes with the news. He told me that Aunt Sophie was going home as soon as he comes back from the hospital with Mom and a surprise for me. First it was a present and now it's a surprise. Dad said he would take me to the hospital when he got Mom but he couldn't because I was too little. I hope he hurries. I really miss my Mom and I can't wait to see my surprise.

Hey, they're pulling in the driveway now. It looks like Mom got rid of her basketball and traded it in for something she's carrying in that white blanket. That must be my surprise.

It's a miniature version of me! I think I'm a lot cuter, though. I hope this is not my surprise. I was hoping for something to play with. This thing is so fragile looking and puny, I'd be afraid I'd break it if I dropped it. Look out kid, Aunt Sophie is coming with one of her sloppy kisses. After this kid gets one of those slobarinos, she probably won't have to go to church and have that bald guy almost drown her in that huge water fountain.

Well Aunt Sophie is leaving. I guess getting this little kid in exchange for her was a good trade.

It looks like Mom is going to change its diaper. I'm almost passed that stage in my life. Pretty soon I'll be going where big people go.

Oh my God! It looks like Mom brought home a defective model. It has something missing in its plumbing area. It doesn't look too upset, but I sure would be.

After Mom changed its diaper she said to me, "Freddie, meet your new sister, Rose."

Sister. That means she's not like me. She's going to look like that pretty redhead who lives down the street, when she gets bigger. What a bummer! I can't play with a girl. This whole day has really gone down the toilet. I think I'd have been a lot happier if Mom and Dad would have brought me home a little dog. Well, Mom's still young yet. There's still time for her to go get me a brother, or a dog.

FREDDIE GETS A PUP

Mom's all excited today because she says Dad is bringing home a puppy. I'm not sure what a puppy is, but I've seen them on TV commercials and they seem awfully noisy to me. Mom and Dad are always telling me to keep quiet because they're trying to get some sleep. Why in the heck would they want to get something that is always making noise? I hope they have a bed for this thing, because he sure isn't sleeping with me. I barely have enough room in bed for myself and all of my toys.

Well, Dad is home and Mom is going bananas. I don't think she got that excited when she brought me home. I figured she would be after carrying me around for nine months. I wonder where they get these pups. Here's Dad, I guess I should act as excited as Mom is. Boy, is he tiny and fuzzy. I wonder why they didn't give him a haircut before Dad picked him up. Hey, I'm calling him a him, when he could be a her—I'll have to check its plumbing when I get down on the floor.

I can't believe the energy this little fart has. He hasn't sat still since he got here. By the way, he is a boy dog—I heard Mom call him Bruce a few minutes ago.

What's Dad putting together? It looks like a portable prison. That better be for Bruce and not for me. I have my own bed and I've heard that saying, "Let sleeping dogs lie." Maybe it should be "Let sleeping dogs lie in their own bed."

Hey, they are putting him in that metal

contraption now, and it looks like he may finally go to sleep. The poor little fart must be exhausted from all the running around he was doing.

Mom told me that after Bruce wakes up I can try to play with him. I wonder what she means, "Try to play with him."

Well, evidently ten minutes is all a pup needs to recharge himself. You ought to see the slop that Mom put in a bowl for him to eat. That stuff isn't suitable for a dog to eat. Hey, I made a funny and I wasn't even trying. He must like it because he gulped it down almost whole. I guess I'll get down on the floor and try to play with him.

Boy, this little fart is nuts—he keeps jumping up on me and running around in circles. I think he likes me. All that jumping around made him pee on Mom's carpet. She grabbed him and said to Dad, "Nice training, Dad." Dad took Bruce off Mom's hands and ran out to the back yard. It looks like he's doing number two on the grass out there. I wonder why Dad didn't take Bruce up to the bathroom on the second floor. Not enough time to get there, I guess.

I'll tell you one thing; they better get out some nail clippers to trim his nails down a little. Those suckers are lethal!

They brought me home a sister, which I never asked for, and now a puppy. Don't I have any rights around this house? I was just starting to get used to a little girl around here and now this, a puppy. It never ends, does it?

Sad Endings

ABDUL

My name is Abdul and I live in a crowded, dilapidated home with my mother, two younger brothers, and one older brother Mohammed. I am fifteen years old. My father was killed two years ago while attempting a robbery. We had no food in our home and he was just trying to provide for our family. Our neighborhood is quite dangerous. Gunfire is heard every night and also frequently during the day. We are not an enemy of the people, but are treated that way.

The local authorities are always questioning us. I know it's because of our race and religion. We live in terror, and are frightened at each knock of our door.

I attend a local school provided by the government. I excel at all my classes and I'm always at the top of my class. My school is also a very frightening place. It receives numerous bomb threats every week and most of the male students carry a gun. I hope to further my education and eventually move from this city. I'd like to get a job where I can receive the respect I know I deserve. My mother wishes I would succeed so I can set an example for my younger brothers.

My mother says that my older brother Mohammed is a lost cause. Like all of his friends Mohammed has an illegal gun and a rifle. My mother told Mohammed that some day he would break her heart because of his political views. That fearful day came yesterday. Mohammed and a few of his friends were killed in a shootout with the local authorities. My mother told the authorities she had no money to bury Mohammed. They said the government would take care of the burial.

You would think from the words I write that I live in Afghanistan, Iraq, or Iran. I don't live in these countries. I live in Chicago, Illinois. You can see a family in Chicago faces the same prejudices and fears as other countries.

DEATH OF A LADY

I met Anne in the summer of 1965 and I knew instantly that I wanted to spend the rest of my short life with her. She lived in a place that her father built in Mt. Washington, a suburb outside of downtown Pittsburgh. She didn't live in the ritzy section of Mt. Washington with the high rises and expensive townhouses, but on a noisy, heavily traveled side street a few blocks from it.

Anne was the spitting image of her mother, with her long legs and beautiful brown eyes. Anne's mom was a sweetheart, but her dad was always yelling or wailing about something. Anne would often be down at the bottom of her street looking out over Mother Nature. She loved the sun, the skies, and the trees. I cautioned her about the dangers of sitting out in the open like she always did. Really though, it wasn't that dangerous. It was my way of offering to protect her while I got to know her personally.

Anne loved seeing movies at the drive-in, but her Mom didn't like her going alone. She worried about it being dark when she had to come home. I offered to accompany Anne to the drive-in. Her Mom agreed but her dad had reservations. I don't think he trusted me. When I promised to bring her home before midnight and stay on the main lighted roads, he agreed. The first time we went to the drive-in we almost got thrown out. I was whistling too much and a lot of the patrons complained that they couldn't hear the movie. Hell, most of them weren't watching the movie anyway. Why did they have to hear it?

I began regularly meeting Anne at the bottom of her street to "protect her." Anne confided in me that her parents were not in the best of health and had indicated they were thinking of moving to Florida. No one else knew this information because of the possibility that her mom and dad's place would be taken over by poachers. Anne told me that she hoped to inherit her parent's place when they made their big move. She wanted it because she said that she wished to have ten or fifteen offspring. This news excited me, and I then made a concerted effort to get her parents out of their place. Anne was the only offspring left because her remaining siblings had left home.

I must really have the gift of gab, because the next day Anne's parents were making preparations for their move to Florida in the fall. They wanted to escape the nasty weather in Pittsburgh immediately.

As I mentioned before, Anne's parents were getting up in age and Florida was pretty far away. A couple of Anne's siblings were already living in Florida, and I'm sure they would put her parents up with them. Five or six of Anne's siblings were getting up in age and agreed to accompany Anne's parents on their long trip to the Sunshine state. They also had enough of the bitter cold and snowy days routinely occurring in Pittsburgh.

Anne and I decided to seal our relationship before her parents flew to Florida. We had the ceremony at a local ball field a few blocks from Anne's house. There must have been two or three hundred in attendance. There was no time for a honeymoon, though. I had to get working on those ten to fifteen offspring. Hell, maybe we'd go for twenty.

Our daily lives were filled with love and Anne and I did everything together. We shopped for food, spent long days at the local park, and played with our offspring. Everyone loved Anne.

The winters in Pittsburgh were brutal, especially those below zero days and nights. Thank God we had compassionate neighbors and benefactors who supplied us with food and drink during those dark times.

We didn't manage the twenty offspring but we did have nineteen. They have all moved out now but some live relatively close to us.

I was coming home one day and I was shocked to see my Anne lying on the ground beneath our home. I talked to her and she told me that she could not move. At first I thought she was attacked by someone or something but she assured me she was just getting old. I tried lying next to her to see if the heat from my body would revitalize her enough for her to get to our home. I'm afraid it didn't work. I think she was getting worse. Soon all of our offspring had heard of their Mom's illness and were by her side. I didn't want to drown her with too much attention, so I assigned them shifts to watch over their sick Mom.

One of our offspring came to me and told me he thought the end was near. I went down to see my Anne, and indeed it was just a matter of time. I spent around two hours with her and she finally expired. I was devastated. I couldn't leave her lying on the ground like that. I gathered all our offspring together and had them find coverings for their Mom. We all said a short prayer and went on our way. She was a great lady and now that lady is dead.

MY BROTHER

I see him every Sunday at the 10 o'clock mass at our neighborhood church. I wonder if he knows he's my half-brother. I almost told him a couple of times, but I was afraid it would cause friction in our families. His older sister knows who I am, but I'm almost positive that he doesn't.

Years ago when my mother was still a teenager, she had an affair with an older married man, my father. That was frowned upon in the mid-forties, but to be pregnant as well was really a no-no. I don't know all the details of my mom's pregnancy, but I do know that she had me at a hospital that is no longer in existence.

My father died ten years ago and I was able to visit him in the hospital before he passed. He died a few weeks after that visit, but I need not dare visit him at the funeral home. His wife hated my mother and I, which in a way, I felt was justified.

In the Catholic Church there is a religious custom that is part of the mass. The celebrating priest would say, "Peace be with you," and we would say, "And with your holy spirit." The priest would then say, "Let us offer each other a sign of peace." Everyone would then shake hands with the person in front of them, behind them, and to each side of them and say, "Peace be with you." In the case of a husband and wife attending mass, they would usually shake hands and kiss affectionately. That is if they were currently speaking to each other, otherwise a hand shake would do.

Sometimes my wife and I would attend different masses, but I usually attended the 10 o'clock. When I attended by myself, I would stand in the back of the church where there was a high wall that people used to lean on. My brother was always standing there for the 10 o'clock mass, and I always stood beside him. For the peace sign I would turn and shake his hand, and say, "Peace be with you," all the while thinking to myself, "Does he know who I am? Should I tell him who I am?"

My mom died a few years ago and I thought seriously of telling my step-brother who I was. Who knows. Maybe he knows already? I'm getting close to seventy years old, so I better hurry up if I'm going to do it. I'm so afraid that he may know and reject me.

This little story started out as a poem titled, "My Sister," in my first book of poetry. I included it in my third book of poetry. Now I have changed the title to "My Brother," and converted into a short story. I'm making some progress; maybe in the next week or two, I'll tell him that we shared the same Father and that I am his half-brother.

OUR FAMILY SECRET

I lived with my mother and older sister Sue. No one ever mentioned my father—for some reason that subject was taboo in our household. My mom died about a week ago when I was approached by Sue. She said, "Robbie, I have some very disturbing news for you—it's time the family closet was opened."

For years we tried to protect you from despair and embarrassment, but now that your grandmother has died, it is time to clear the air. Yes, she was your grandmother, not your mother as you had thought. I am your birth mother. I know this startling news will shock and confuse you. You see, I was violated years ago by someone I will not name. He was not a family member as is the case in many rapes.

Your grandparents sent me away to your Aunt Margaret's to hide the pregnancy from our small town. They didn't want our family to suffer any humiliation and shame. Your grandmother was a great actress and I hid my pregnancy well. Your father died years ago and has surely gone to hell as he was not a nice or good man.

There are skeletons in many closets and I'm glad that ours is finally out. This secret has weighed heavily on my heart over the years, and I hope now that we can live a normal life, although there is one more secret involving your grandfather. I will wait a while to reveal that news to you. I think you've heard enough family news for one day.

THE BLOODY HATS

I decided to write this little story after seeing a picture of a pile of bloody hats in my daily newspaper. They were remnants of a suicide bomber's handy work.

This was not an Army-Navy game where the participants throw their hats into the air usually signifying the end of the game. These hats were not signifying the end of a battle, but the end of people's lives contributing to a so-called Holy War. There were 52 dead and over 250 wounded, most of them critically. These lives were taken as they prayed to God with thanks.

This was another suicide bombing where no one is safe. The bomber provided an expressway to heaven as its victim's lives on earth are taken away. The bomber thinks that this action will provide him with an afterlife of everlasting joy, but in reality it provides him or her with a quick pass to the Devil's door, where they will be welcomed with open arms to suffer in everlasting fire.

When those hats were thrown into the air they were supposed to signify a victory for the winning team, but they actually are a symbol of death's gruesome scene.

THE BLOODY TENNIES

It was a cold and rainy night, and I dread the thought of walking down that long winding road. It has been raining for days and it's actually easier to walk down that hill than trying to drive it.

It's getting late and I hope that little liquor store is still open. I need another bottle of booze to help me sleep tonight. It was nice of my brother to let me hide out here. The two grand in cash I gave him may have swayed his decision though. I'm loaded and he's dirt poor. He never could hang onto is money.

Let's start with why I'm here.

My wife and I had a combative marriage. We were happy at one time, but over the years we seemed to drift apart. She recently informed me that she was filing for a divorce. I could not afford a divorce. Well, maybe I could, but I like my money too well. My friends and relatives all say that they've never, in their lives, seen a cheaper individual than me. That's why my wife must die. I'm not sharing any of my money with anyone, especially her. I think I may have a little love for her, but not enough love not to kill her. Thank God you can still hide your money in a Swiss bank, which is exactly what I did. After I killed my wife I plan on laying low at my brother's cabin and then take a plane overseas until I can make arrangements to get my money. I invested wisely and I have plenty of funds to live out my life in semi-luxury.

I wouldn't get into the details of the murder

except to tell you that it was extremely bloody. I never knew that one gunshot would result in so much gun splatter. I cleaned the murder scene the best that I could and then started on my drive to my brother's cabin.

I had been to this cabin once before and remembered how muddy the road going up was. With the rain we had that night, I barely made it. The first thing I did when I got to the cabin was burn the clothes I was wearing when I committed the murder. I looked around and found a loose floorboard in my closet. Tennis shoes don't burn well, so I figured I would hide them there.

Now we are back to me walking down that messy hill for a bottle of hooch. As I was walking toward the front door I looked down and remembered I was wearing my new pair of tennis shoes. I paid almost three-hundred dollars for these puppies and there's no way I'm going to trench through that mud. I decided to go in the floorboard and pull out the tennies I was wearing at the time of the murder. When I retrieved them I got a better look at them. There was quite a lot of blood still on them, even though I thought I cleaned them pretty well. One trip through the mud wouldn't hurt these.

The little trip through that slop didn't take long. I guess it was only a fourth of a mile or so.

Thank God the lights are on in the liquor store. I could use that bourbon now. As I entered the store a huge cop was staring at me. I tried to walk past him, but then he said, "Stop where you are, mister. I just saw your picture on my mobile APB." Modern technology has been my undoing. I found out after my arrest that the police suspected me and e-mailed my photo to the local authorities. From searching my home they discovered the town where my brother's cabin was located. They included my photo in the town's police network, and that's how the policeman recognized me. How ironic can this be? I'll probably spend the next thirty years in prison for murdering my wife because I didn't want to get my new tennies dirty!

There's another bit of irony to this story. A couple of weeks before my wife died, and with my brother's authorization, I was made legal guardian of all his monetary assets if he was unable to maintain them.

Through the course of the trial it was revealed that the person who called to report my wife's murder was my brother. When the police arrived he also told them that I may be hiding out at his cabin.

I guess that money is more important than brotherly love to him.

THE PAINTING

My name is John Speakman and I've lived in this small fishing village of Andara, where I offer fishing trips for a living, on the west coast of Ireland for most of my seventy-eight years. I've never married and all of my relatives have left this world. I am a quiet, non-drinking man who doesn't enjoy many of what people consider the finer things of life, except fishing and observing fine art. To me, they are the finer things in my life.

Being from Andara has allowed me to pursue my passion for fishing. It also allows me to observe art in various forms. There are many galleries in town that display art, and for such a small village, we have a good share of them. The reason for this is the wild and deserted landscapes of glens, moors, lakes, and our numerous waterfalls. They provide artists with the beauty to transfer from their eyes to canvases and other painting surfaces.

After an enjoyable day of fishing on Monday, my only free day, I usually stop home, clean up, and head to town to observe the current art that the many galleries have to offer. I've taken tourists on fishing trips so many times that I instantly recognize a location the artists have painted. I enjoy going to these galleries to see the different interpretations of scenes the various artists create. Typically, the same location will appear in a couple different galleries. I've been to and seen most of the locations the local and visiting artists have painted, until now.

I observed this new painting in one of the galleries I regularly visit. It was a painting of a fisherman done in various shades of blue. It looks as though the man was fishing in a small, isolated lake with pools of swirling water. The scene was serene: a boat and a man in his paradise, without a care in the world. I had to find this place. I'm sure it is somewhere in the village.

I asked the gallery owner, Kevin Kilcary, if he could tell me who had submitted this painting. He said that the painter was a man of the cloth, Father James Julius, from Calabria, Italy. Usually the artists submit at least four or five paintings on a consignment basis. Father Julius had only submitted one. It was appropriately titled, "Paradise." Father Julius told Kevin he would return to the village in a few months to see if anyone had purchased it. I told Kevin to let me know when the good Father returned because I wanted to find out where it was painted. In the mean time, I would search the village to find the location where the Father painted this bit of artistic excellence.

It became an obsession, finding the location of that painting. My every waking moment became consumed with trying to find the location depicted in the painting. It was starting to affect my health. I began experiencing a shortness of breath as well as a deep burning sensation in my chest. The village doctor, Simon Seleski, told me these occurrences were probably brought on from stress. I knew it was the stress of not finding that location. Dr. Seleski suggested I try and take it easy and not spend so much time worrying about the painting and where it was painted. He also suggested I find a phone number or e-mail for Father Julius and inquire about the painting. I explained to him that I had Kevin Kilcary try both of those avenues to try to contact the Father. The doctor was informed by the Father's superiors that Father Julius traveled quite a bit and would be back in Andara in a few months.

After a few months of searching, with no luck, I received a phone call from Kevin at the gallery. He told me Father Julius had visited the gallery that day and would return the following morning at 10AM to have a short meeting with me. Kevin explained that Father Julius was currently working at the Vatican for a few months and had explained the circumstances of why I wanted to meet with him. Kevin told me that Father Julius told him where he painted "Paradise," but would tell me at our meeting the following morning. Paradise; it was the first time I heard the name of the painting. I had never bothered to inquire about the title and it was never displayed with the painting. "That title seems appropriate", I thought to myself.

I didn't sleep a wink that night wondering what news I would hear the next day. Our meeting was scheduled for ten in the morning, but I was there at nine. I went to the painting and stared at it. It gave me a feeling of ease throughout my body. It was an eerie but enjoyable feeling.

Just then, I felt a hand on my shoulder. I turned and observed a small man dressed in priestly garb. "I talked to Kevin, and I assume you are John Speakman. I'm Father Julius and I'm sorry for all the trouble I have caused you. You see, the reason you can't find the location in the village of where I painted 'Paradise' is because it wasn't painted here. Last year I had a vision of the image you see in that painting. Most people would call it a dream. In this vision an angel told me to paint what I had seen and take it to your village. The angel said the painting would be directly responsible for impacting someone's life. In the morning I immediately painted what I had remembered in my vision."

I thanked Father Julius for the information and my mind seemed immediately at ease. Father again apologized for causing me trouble and said he was sorry that he had to leave so quickly , before telling me it was a pleasure meeting me. He said he had to catch a flight back to Rome.

After he left I returned to the painting, yet again. I stared at it and couldn't get over how great it made me feel. I led a dull existence, but fishing and observing art seemed to lift my spirits. I looked at the fisherman in the painting again and observed how he seemed to be so at peace. I studied the water again and thought how calm and cool it seemed. I thought about what Father Julius said, "The painting would be directly responsible for someone's life." Just then I felt a burning pain deep in my chest, but instead of falling back, I was drawn toward the wall where the painting was.

I won't have to worry about visiting the gallery and observing the painting anymore because now the fisherman in the painting was me.

When Father Julius mentioned that the painting would be responsible for someone's life—what it meant was, it would be responsible for someone's renewed life in "Paradise."

THE MYSTERY FLIGHT

After a long fight with cancer, my wife of forty years passed away. We received the customary three opinions, but the diagnosis was always the same: inoperative ovarian cancer.

Jeanie believed in the hereafter. The closer she got to death the more she talked about it.

She frequently told me, "I am going to another time, and I will make sure that you are in that time."

I entertained her fantasy. I knew all the drugs she was taking were surely affecting her mind and reasoning. When she talked about her hereafter it seemed to perk her up, and it helped her pass the time.

Jeanie wanted to die in our home. Near the end she had hospice nurses attending her needs every day. We still had our nights and we would reminisce and speak of our lives together.

I was not a completely faithful husband. In our forty years of marriage I had six affairs. I thought about confessing to Jeanie, but felt there wouldn't be any point in it. I could see no reason for her to take those facts with her. I was very discreet in my affairs, and Jeanie had no idea I had ever been unfaithful. At least I thought as much.

The hospice nurse told me it was a matter of days until my Jeanie's death. While talking to her that night, she could tell I had heard some disturbing news. She made me promise when I knew her death was near that I would tell her.

That night she said, "You remember your promise, don't you? How much time do I have?"

"The nurse said possibly a month at the most," I said.

Jeanie told me she had been thinking about her hereafter more and more and said she knew of a way that I could also go. "I've come up with a phrase for you to look for. The phrase will be: Jeanie's calling, and she's ready Jack."

I continued to amuse her and said, "Yes my dear, I will be looking for that phrase."

Jeanie died ten days later and I held as beautiful a funeral as I could for her. It was hard to believe she was gone. I casually thought to myself, "I guess I better start looking for that phrase."

It had been a couple days since my Jeanie died. I thought I'd check to see if I'd received any mail. The mail typically seemed to be junk mail and various bills. But there it was, a letter addressed to me in my wife's handwriting, and there was no postmark on the letter. I told no one of Jeanie's delusions, so I was puzzled. Who could have placed this letter in my mail box? I started to shake all over. Was Jeanie's plan becoming a reality? I cautiously opened the letter and there it was in large printed red letters, "Jeanie's calling, and she's ready Jack." I almost passed out, feverishly grasping for air. I was shaking so much I was dangerously close to falling out of the chair. I thought to myself, "Maybe this is a bad dream, but it seemed so real." In the letter was an airline ticket and an additional sheet of paper with instructions for me. The destination on the ticket read, "Unknown." The additional sheet of paper was also in Jeanie's handwriting and read, "I know you are shocked Jack, but you must follow my instructions 'To the T' for this to work."

I didn't know what to do so I decided to get my affairs in order, just in case I wasn't coming back. I thought, "What are you getting yourself into, Jack? You should just burn this letter and get on with your life." But then a crazy thought entered my mind, "Maybe this is for real. I'm getting up in years and there aren't many left. Maybe I'll take a shot at this craziness."

Jeanie's instructions said to bring no luggage. I drove to the airport, anticipating my trip. Don't ask me why, but I parked in the short-term lot. I went directly to the list of departing flights after entering the airport. On the schedule was a departure listed as "Unknown," and the flight was to depart in only a few minutes, so I knew I'd better get moving. There was a plane on the runway with huge writing on the side of it. It read, "Jeanie's calling, and she's ready Jack." This seemed to be getting more real every minute.

I arrived at the departure gate where a female attendant was standing. "Oh, so you're Jack. Jeanie is waiting for you."

She had a devilish grin on her face while she spoke to me. In fact, if you'd put a set of horns on her head, she could have passed for the devil himself. I walked up the steps to the cabin and entered. When I arrived in the cabin, I began to perspire profusely and wondered if I was having a heart attack. I felt an extraordinary amount of heat and a colossal wall of fire. I thought, "What the hell is going on? Is this my wife's gift to me for all my indiscretions?" Just then, a deep gravely voice found its way through the fire. It said, "You should have resisted your adulteress desires."

I tried desperately to wake up. All of this had to be a bad dream. I prayed to God, "Please let me wake up". I woke up and realized that I was definitely having a nightmare, but where was all this heat coming from? I quickly realized I had been smoking in bed again and that the bedroom was on fire. I desperately tried to get out of my bed, but the intense fire was beginning to consume me. I heard sirens and women screaming outside my window. I realized then that I wasn't in my bedroom. I was in another place. I realized the women screaming were not outside my house, but were in the room with me. Through the fire I recognized them. They were the women I had my affairs with. They were screaming from the intense heat. I finally accepted the fact that this was not a dream, and that I would spend all of eternity in this hell.

I recalled what Jeanie said to me, "I am going to another time, and I will make sure that you are in that time." Ironically I was in that time with Jeanie, but I wasn't in the same place.

THE ROOM

My grandfather built this house around the early 1900's. It was a large red brick with a wrap around porch which was utilized by the whole family through the years. The house was located at the edge of a small Midwestern town in the state of Georgia. In its day it was quite charming, but over the years it has become quite run down. One of the main reasons for its poor condition was the lack of help to do needed maintenance and repair work. The war had taken all of our able bodied men. The house had two large bedrooms, though actually there used to be three. I took over the third bedroom of which only I had a key.

I would visit this room once a year and spend an hour or two in it, always having a tear in my eye when exiting. Visiting relatives would ask about the room, especially my cousin, Amy. Every time Amy inquired about the room, I would tell her, "I may die before you, Amy, and if I do, I will make sure you get the key, to satisfy your curiosity."

In my day, I was quite the looker, but no one ever saw me with a man. I would always say I guessed a husband was not in God's plan for me.

My mother died at a young age and my father suffered from chronic diabetes, which eventually confined him to a wheelchair. He died last year, blind and crippled. He was a good man and I don't know why God chose him to suffer .

Most of my days, and many nights, were consumed taking care of the house and my father.

Now that he is gone I don't know what I'll do with myself. I am not very healthy myself, having inherited my mother's heart condition. I think the yearly visits to The Room probably helped in my debilitating condition of my heart.

I received some sad and startling news from my heart doctor yesterday. It appears I have a valve in my heart that has deteriorated to the point that if it collapses fully, I will lose my ability to breathe. The doctor told me this could occur at any time and said I could live another year, or another month, or another day. He said this condition was difficult to predict.

When I arrived home, I immediately called my cousin Amy and said I wanted her to come over because I had news for her. I told her it was time I gave her the key to The Room and added, "There will be an envelope taped to my front door for you."

Amy was excited with the news that I gave her, but didn't seem too worried about my well being. I think she was looking forward to seeing what was in the room more than the outcome of the condition of my health.

I prepared an envelope that held an explanation for Amy regarding what The Room was all about. After I had written the lengthy letter, I taped it to my front door. I wasn't feeling too well and decided I would make an unscheduled visit to The Room. It was the first time in forty years that I did not visit the room on the anniversary of what was a very sad day in my life. As I entered, I felt something in my chest. I turned on the only light, sat in the only chair there, and died.

For someone who, over the years, couldn't wait to find out what was in the room, Amy sure seemed to take her time. She arrived about an hour later and saw the letter taped to the front door. She immediately sat in one of the porch's lounge chairs, opened the letter, and began reading. The letter read:

Amy, as you read this I may be near death or already there. I know you were looking forward to seeing what was in "The Room." One thing I would ask of you is to read this letter to the end until you use the key to open The Room.

While on a two week vacation in Atlantic City several years ago, I met a man. We met on the boardwalk, we dated, one thing led to another, and we fell in love. He was on a vacation, like me, before he was to be inducted into the U.S. Marines. After his basic training in Louisiana, he was issued orders to be sent somewhere in Europe. Where exactly, he didn't know.

We decided to marry when he came home, when the war was over.

They were uncertain times then, and you had to prepare your life for anything. I prepared for my fiancée to come home, both of us getting married, and planned living a life of joy and happiness with my husband.

When I arrived home from Atlantic City, I decided to drive to Augusta and purchase a wedding dress for this happiest time of my life. I told no one of my engagement, or the wedding dress. As I said previously, those were uncertain times, and I didn't want anyone feeling sorry for me if for some reason our wedding plans did not work out.

As it turns out, our plans didn't materialize.

I had a post office box set up in our little town to receive letters from Joe. One day I received a letter that I didn't recognize the handwriting of; I knew it wasn't Joe's. It was from a close friend of his who was serving with him in Europe. It appears that Joe was killed on a beach called Omaha. At the time I had never heard of this beach. All I know was that my love was dead and I began entertaining thoughts of ending my own life. My religious upbringing prevented me from doing that though, so I lived my life with the private memory of Joe.

I had hidden the wedding dress well in my room. One day while cleaning I devised the idea for The Room. The only thing in The Room was a worn buttoned black leather chair and an old brass pole lamp, and of course, my wedding dress. I would visit The Room once a year on the anniversary of Joe's death, cry uncontrollably, and think of how things could have been.

That's what the big mystery of The Room, was all about. I hope I fulfilled your expectations with what was in there: a wedding dress. You may now take the key, open The Room, call the coroners, and see to it that I get a proper burial.

Your cousin,
Mary

THE SIGNAL

I've been married to my wife, Jean, for fourteen years. The first ten years were great, but the last four have been a nightmare. We just don't seem to agree on anything anymore. I know this may sound a little conceited, but in most cases I'm usually right, and she is usually wrong. This has made for a rocky situation. I can only stay out and drink so long; my liver is taking a beating. Jean entertains her friends with most of her spare time and has just recently taken up crocheting. I'm glad that she has found a hobby, but buying the yarn is costing me a fortune. Jean works part-time at a local convenience store and I'm a registered plumber who works out of the local union hall.

I first met Rita at the local Eagles club, where we hit it off immediately. Rita is also married and lives a similar life as I do. She is a beautiful and passionate woman whose cheats on her husband. I don't know why she cheats, but for my sake I'm glad she does. Rita and I would have our little encounters at the local Motel 6, or even in the back seat of my car, occasionally. I make good money when I work, but I also spend a lot of it too. Motel 6 is the cheapest lodging in our small town, but even with their low rates, meeting up with Rita is costing me an arm and a leg. I guess I could ask Rita to pay every once in a while, but I'm afraid she'd dump me.

We talked it over one night and decided to meet at her house for our little get-togethers. We decided we could do this because Rita's husband was out every night. Rita had a nice, small, ranch home with a detached garage. I could never tell if her husband's car was in the garage or not. Rita and I decided we needed a signal to show if her husband, George, was home or not. We settled on the lit candle in the front window scenario. If it was lit that meant George was out and it was safe for me to enter her house. By the way, the front door was always open.

I wonder where George goes at night when he should be home with such a beautiful woman. Who knows. He could be having his own little get-together.

Well, this little arrangement had worked out well for around six months. I'm glad we thought of it, and I'm saving a lot of money on motel bills. I dread the thought of getting caught. George seems a wimpy guy, but I understand he studied karate and has a black belt, whatever that is. So I may have a hard time kicking his butt if I get caught with Rita.

Well, wouldn't you know it; I hear the garage door opening. I asked Rita why George would be coming home so early. She told me that he wasn't feeling well lately and he may be sick, and was coming home early to go to bed.

I got all my belongings together as fast as I could and told Rita I would call her the following day and set up our next rendezvous. I always parked my car about a block away from Rita's place in case George happened to drive by. It was early, but as usual, I was short on cash. I decided to go home and see what Jean does all those nights I'm not home. I figured she was probably crocheting something.

As I approached my garage I saw a familiar looking car, but I couldn't remember where I saw it. Then I remembered that it was George's car. I parked my vehicle and approached the front door of my house. In the bay window stood a large white candle, lit of course. Well now I know what George was doing every night when he should have been home with his wife. He was with mine. Oh, the nerve!

THE STRANGER

I thought I would go for a drive. I was thinking about my recently deceased wife and how much I missed her. It was raining pretty hard and sometimes a drive in that kind of rain would pick me up.

After driving a few miles, I spotted a hitchhiker. I didn't think that people hitched rides today with the state our country is in; there are too many wackos out there. I guess he was pretty desperate with the way the rain was coming down. He looked pretty safe, I suppose they always do, but for some strange reason I felt myself drawn to him. I talked to him for a bit and found I was going in his direction. He couldn't thank me enough for the ride.

We made small talk for a while and then the conversation shifted to my life. It seemed kind of strange that he knew so many personal things about my life, especially the recent loss of my wife from her long battle with cancer. All of a sudden his voice changed dramatically.

He said, "I am an angel from God and I'm here to take you to the Lord."

"I don't think I'm ready to go, I'd really like to stay here," I replied.

"I'm very sorry, my friend, but the Lord has instructed me to take you to your new forever home." As we continued to drive along, I heard the strangest sound and felt a floating sensation inside my chest. I realized that I was no longer on the ground but flying upward toward the skies. As we were raised higher at an accelerated speed, I noticed a very bright light ahead of us. I felt a chill all over my body. It was not a cold chill, though. It's hard to explain, but it made me feel the happiest and safest I've ever felt in my life.

I looked over and my angel said, "This is as far as I go, my friend. My Lord has more like you that I have to release from their life on earth. There are many, like you, who don't know that the Lord has sent a messenger to take them to His home."

As I lost sight of my angel I felt my body shed and the only thing left of me was my soul.

I realized I was in paradise. All of my loved ones who had passed before me were now in my afterlife. I know now why I lived such a sin-free life; it's because I wanted to live a life of love for my Lord, forever.

THE WAITRESS

I've been doing this job for fifteen years now, and it's really what I want to do the rest of my life. I work in a beautiful house of white and sky blue. I love all the beautiful people who visit my house. I am a waitress in this huge house and I do my best to take care of my customer's needs. I offer a limited menu. In fact, I only offer one thing, and that is memories. These are memories that have been lost in my customer's minds. These memories are served in the form of faces and places that have been forgotten for a long time. I serve these memory meals on a platter of time. I love to see the joy on my customer's faces when they realize that I have brought them a renewal of the life that they had forgotten.

The people who frequent my house are special people, and they all share a terrible decease: Alzheimer's. It is different from other diseases' that can cripple the body—Alzheimer's cripples your mind.

My house is a temporary stop until they reach the highest parts of heaven. The suffering they endured on earth will be replaced with memories of joy and everlasting life. I know I will not have this job forever, for like other human diseases, God will provide a cure. I thank God for this opportunity to help these people and I look forward to meeting them again in God's world.

THE WHITE DOOR

I had a long tiring day at work today and I couldn't wait to lay my head on that overstuffed pillow of mine. I think I'm even going to skip dinner.

I've been having some goofy dreams lately. Hopefully because I'm so tired I'll be able to sleep through the night. I'm feeling a little odd and I can't explain it. Maybe if I get to sleep all these weird thoughts and feelings will be gone in the morning. I normally fall asleep watching David Letterman, but tonight I think I'll put Conan on. That would put Cinderella to sleep.

I must have dozed off when I felt a strong force grabbing my body and I was swiftly pulled from my bed. I wondered if this was another one of those weird dreams I've been having lately, but I didn't remember any of them being this physical. I felt alive, but I could very well be dead. I've never felt this strange in my life, that is if I'm still alive.

The next thing I knew, this force had me traveling at lightning speed, and I wondered if this frightening journey would ever end. Ahead of me I saw a brilliant shining light. It was as bright as the sun, but I knew it couldn't be the sun, because if it was, there would be an unbearable heat along with it. But if I'm dead I wouldn't feel any heat, would I? I wish this dream would be over already, because it's driving me crazy.

As I neared the bright light, I felt my body holding back, but my mind was telling me to ascend. I entered the bright light and I felt my body shedding away. This may be the most realistic dream I've ever been in. I felt like a captive, but at the same time I felt very free.

As my now fascinating journey continued, I was introduced to beautiful transparent colors in the form of small clouds. The colors were in a swirling motion with small puffy clouds of white enveloped between the new colors I was being introduced to.

In the distance I could see a long winding path with large white doves all around. I assume they were there to lead the way. If this was just a dream, as I was hoping, I wondered how long my mind would be captured by this entity. I very much wanted to awaken but I was curious as to what was at the end of that long path. I approached the doves and I could tell that they were communicating with my mind—they wanted me to follow them.

As I neared the end of the path the dove somehow disappeared. I don't even know when or how they disappeared; all of a sudden they were not there.

At the end of the path was a humongous white door with images of all the friends and relatives who died before me, if I am in fact dead. The immenseness of this door enabled me to recognize all the faces. There were some prominent faces I could not see, so I assumed they went to the other place.

I can be downright hard-headed at times but I finally had to admit to myself I had entered the hereafter, and was about to become one of God's team. This is all I'm going to tell you at this time. You know that no one has ever came back from death and told you of the huge white door. I suggest that if you are not living your life according to God's rules, you change as soon as you can, and your image will appear on the white door.

WILL

No one knows much about the man who lived in this small cottage. Most of the old timers say he moved there after World War II.

The vine covered cottage is at the top of a long, winding, unpaved road. There is an electrified fence surrounding the property at the base of the hill. There are "No Trespassing" signs attached to the fence at five foot intervals. Under each sign is another indicating the danger of electrocution if the fence is touched or tampered with.

It is possible to see the cottage from any watercraft, although anyone wishing to see it clearly would need binoculars. The cottage overlooks the Pacific Ocean in this small coastal city in southern California. There is a huge open deck overlooking the ocean and there were no chairs or tables on the deck. During the day you can see various sizes of what appears to be paintings on easels. You can barely see windows on the sides of the cottage because they are mostly obscured by a crawling green vine. I imagine with the breath taking view from its deck, there was no reason to sit behind windows.

I have lived in this community of Lamoines, California for six years and the population is 20,000. It is a lovely city with many small homes and cottages. Most of the properties are used by vacationers, but there are some permanent residents living there, like myself. My name is Joe Black, and I am the Lamoines Chief of Police. I retired from the Los Angeles Police Department after twenty-five years and moved to Lamoines. The city of Lamoines is relatively crime free. We have a small bank, a service station, a food market, and assorted specialty shops. It was in one of these shops that I first met Will Charles.

Will was a towering man with a huge beer belly. He had a long red beard that reached to his waist. If Will spoke two sentences to you, that was a lot.

The town had a frame and paint shop called Ritter's. It was a small shop, but well stocked. Ritter's was not too far from Los Angeles, so if you needed a special order item, it only took a few days to obtain it.

I spotted Will's cottage one day while sailing. I asked the locals if they knew anything about Will. They all agreed that he was somewhat of a loner and that he had moved to the cottage after WWII was over. They also told me that every other Saturday, without fail, Will would pay a visit to Ritter's.

I asked Jim Ritter if he knew anything about Will and he said he didn't. Jim told me that when Will came to his shop he would buy oil paints and canvases. Jim said, "I asked Will one day what he was painting up at his cottage."

He said Will gave him a dirty look and said, "I don't think it is really any of your business." Jim said he never asked Will about his painting again.

That electrified fence came to my mind and I thought there may be an occasion where I may have to visit Will's cottage. I thought I would call Will and ask him about the possibility of coming to visit his cottage. I checked the local phone directory and found no listing for Will Charles. I assumed the kind of person that Will seemed to be may have an unlisted number. I called the phone company and was told they had no listing for a Will Charles. I decided to wait at Ritter's the following Saturday when Will came in to shop and ask him about his phone number. When Will entered Ritter's I introduced myself.

Will asked me why I was bothering him, saying that he had done nothing wrong.

I told him I knew he had done nothing wrong, but I was concerned about his electrified fence. I told him that we had a dangerous situation there. While I was talking to him I wondered to myself, "Is that fence just for privacy, or is he hiding something." I told Will I might visit him one day.

He repeated, "I have done nothing wrong. There is no reason you would have to visit me."

I said, "Perhaps there could be a fire or you became ill. How would the fire department or medics enter your property with the fence situation?" This must have struck a cord.

Will said, "You may be right; I would not want anything to happen to my life's work."

I asked Will if he had a solution for our dilemma. Will said he would tell me, and only me, how to disarm his electrified fence. I told Will that I trusted my deputy, and he should also know how to disarm the fence in case I wasn't available. Will reluctantly agreed with me.

From my conversation with Will I realized he was a loner like many locals had said, but he also appeared to be a very private and sincere man.

I thanked Will for his cooperation and told him I would see him again someday.

He said, "God, I hope not." I assumed I witnessed an attempt at humor from Will.

After Will left, Jim Ritter called me over. He said, "Boy, you must have a way with people. I've never heard that many words come out of that man's mouth since he started shopping here."

A few months later I received a call from Jim and he sounded a little worried. He told me that Will had not visited his shop for the past two Saturdays, which was extremely unusual.

I thanked him for the information, and said I would check things out. My deputy and I headed for Will's cottage. I'm glad I had that little conversation with Will about his electrified fence, otherwise I don't know what I would have done. We arrived at Will's property and performed the disarming procedure on the electrified fence.

The road up to the cottage was in poor condition. It was clear why Will owned a Jeep. Thankfully I had a four-wheel drive vehicle as well. The cottage appeared to be in pristine condition. There were red roses decorating the front yard. I knocked on the front door but there was no answer. I tried the front door and it was open. When I entered the cottage I couldn't believe my eyes. There were paintings of the same woman everywhere. She appeared to be in her early twenties, had blond hair, and was quite beautiful.

I entered into the living room and looked to the left at what appeared to be a den. It was difficult to tell with all the portraits hanging on the walls which room was what. There was a small desk in this room with more of the same portraits. I proceeded to what I assumed was Will's bedroom. There were more portraits covering these walls as well. I left the bedroom and walked through a long hall that led to the kitchen. There were portraits covering these walls as well. There were even four portraits on the ceiling of the hall.

I entered the kitchen and saw Will sitting at a table. It seemed that Will had been dead for awhile, and that rigor mortis had set in. Naturally the stench of death was quite sharp. Will had paint in front of him and I assumed that he was mixing it in preparation to start another portrait. I didn't realize it when I first entered the kitchen, but there were no portraits on any of these walls.

My deputy entered the kitchen and said, "Look what I've found."

It was a small binder labeled "In case of emergency." I considered this an emergency, so I opened it up. There were about twenty pages in the binder, and there were four lines written on the first page. The first line read, "Will's sister," followed by her street address, city and state, and a phone number. There was also a small white envelope marked "Personal," and addressed to a Janet Meeks.

I called the coroner because I naturally wanted to determine the cause of Will's. Eventually the coroner determined that Will died of a massive heart attack. He told me that all the cigarettes and alcohol found in the cottage may have been a determining factor. I called Will's sister the following day and informed her of her brother's death. She told me that she had not talked to

Will for at least fifteen years and that she would be flying into Lamoines the following morning to meet me.

We had a small airport in Lamoines. Most people took a shuttle from the LA airport. I told Will's sister I would meet her at the airport and drive her into town. There were only ten passengers on the shuttle. I assumed with the uniform I was wearing that Janet would recognize me. As the passengers entered the airport one woman walked up to me and said, "Hello, I'm Janet Meeks, Will's sister. I assume you're Sheriff Black."

I introduced myself, and again offered my condolences for her brother. I handed Janet the envelope that I found in Will's binder. Janet asked me if there was a hotel in town because she planned on staying a few days to get Will's affairs in order.

I told her we had a small, but clean hotel. I then told Janet about the portraits in the cottage.

She told me that when she got settled in the hotel she would visit me at the station. She said, "I will explain everything to you." I couldn't wait to find out the details of Will's obsession.

Janet came to the station a few hours later. She was an attractive woman who looked nothing like her brother. Of course with the long beard and excessive weight on Will, I guess it was hard to tell they were related.

Janet sat down in my office and began the story. "Will was stationed in England during WWII and met the girl in the portrait when he was over there. Her name was Diana, and Will was deeply in love with her. They were planning to be married. Diana was killed in an air raid, and Will was devastated. Will wanted her body brought to the States, but her family would not hear of it. Diana's body was buried in a small local cemetery under a beautiful Aspen tree. "Will was studying art when he was drafted. After the war he resumed his studies. Our parents were quite wealthy and they bought that cottage for Will. I asked Will if I could visit the cottage some time and he told me he'd rather I not. He said he preferred to live his life with himself and the memory of Diana. It's hard to believe he spent the remainder of his life painting portraits of Diana. I guess his love for her turned into an obsession."

Janet asked if I noticed anything odd about the portraits.

I said, "Not really."

Then she said, "If you look at them closely you'll notice that the portraits age. I mean Diana's face gradually ages like she would look today."

I told Janet I was so surprised at the quantity of the pictures that I never noticed that her face had aged. I guess Will believed that Diana was still with him, so he painted her as he thought she would age with him.

I asked Janet if she had thought about any funeral arrangements.

She told me that after I called her about Will's death she contacted Diana's cousin Beth, in England. Beth was familiar with Will and knew of his and Diana's marriage plans during the war. Janet said apparently Will had contacted Beth a few years earlier. Will told Beth that if anything should happen to him his sister Janet would be contacting her to express his desire to be buried next to Diana. I guess fate had stepped in because when Beth checked with the cemetery, she found out that the plot next to Diana's was still available.

Janet made arrangements with the coroner to have her brother's body picked up and then taken directly to the Los Angeles Airport and then flown to England.

I guess in Will's mind Diana was always with him. Now he will be with her forever. He will be with her forever lying next to her under that beautiful Aspen tree.

A FACE IN THE WINDOW

There is a huge corner house in this small southern town of Bentley, SC that has been condemned for many years. The locals claim it is haunted and all but one window is boarded up. If you look toward that window between 3 and 3:15 in the afternoon every day you'll hear crying and see a grown woman appear. Most of the older residents assume it was Mary Roan, the former owner of the house. She lived there with her daughter, Sarah. Sarah disappeared between 3 and 3:15 after getting off her school bus on a bright spring afternoon.

The house is presently owned by a local real estate company. After many attempts they have been unable to keep that window boarded up and there continues to be an image at the window with a low crying voice. Whenever the window is boarded up by the real estate company, the following day it is open again, without any signs of anyone breaking or entering the house.

A lot of the current residents don't remember the day Sarah was abducted, but I remember it well; it was the talk of the town. Many residents moved out of town when this happened. The abductor was never caught, and some people thought he or she may have still lived, or resided outside of Bentley.

I remember the day that Sarah was abducted because I was the one who abducted her. The authorities assumed that Sarah went with someone she thought she could trust; they were right. I was a substitute school teacher at Sarah's school and I taught her class many times.

Sarah was enrolled in a special education program. Considering the size of Bentley, we were lucky we even had a public school. Sarah's mother took her to Raleigh to be tested when she was young. It appeared Sarah was not able to utilize all of her faculties and there wasn't anything they could do to improve her learning capacity. The people in Raleigh wanted Sarah to attend a special school, but Mary had neither the time nor money to do this for her daughter. It was decided Sarah should attend Bentley public school. There were teachers who offered to work with Sarah and try to get her at least an 8th grade diploma.

I had planned my abduction of Sarah very well. I even purchased a home a couple hundred miles from Bentley for Sarah and I to live in. It was at the end of a long street with an enclosed fence around the perimeter. I intended on home schooling Sarah. You may think I am a pedophile, but I am not. I was married for twenty-five years but never had a child since my husband didn't want any children. I should have gotten out of my marriage after the first ten years when he told me, but it was too late to start over. My husband died young and I decided then that somehow I was going to have a child. I thought a long time about abducting Sarah and the consequences if I were to get caught. How could I take a child away from her mother? In my mind I realized that my need was much greater then her loss would be.

I sold my house in Bentley and had a garage sale for anything else I could sell. I gave what I couldn't sell to the Salvation Army. I had my retirement checks forwarded to a post office box in the town where I purchased my new home. I rented a car from Raleigh in case someone saw me take Sarah and recognized my car. I was ready to put my plan into effect.

I parked the rental under a tree about a half of a block from Sarah's stop. It was a Monday, but the abduction could occur any day that week. I had to make sure that Sarah was walking home alone, and was not with any of her friends. I thought about what to say to Sarah that would make her come with me and get into my car. I decided to tell her something happened to her mother and I was going to take her to the hospital to see her.

It was Monday morning when Sarah got off the bus alone. I checked the streets for other cars or people; all was clear. I was very nervous and I had to hurry because Sarah's house was only two short blocks away. Sarah was reluctant at first but she eventually agreed to go with me. She cried the first hour that she was with me and I really felt bad about myself. How could I do something so evil and so cruel; I will surely rot in hell. Eventually I told Sarah that her mother had died. It was about a week after we moved into our new home. I also told her that some day she would meet her mother in a better place. I couldn't believe how easily she accepted this news.

Sarah and I lived in our home for about fifteen years. I only went out to purchase groceries and general things that were needed to maintain a house. I taught Sarah as much as I could academically. She was very good at painting and cutting the grass.

One morning Sarah awoke with a terrible fever and was shaking uncontrollably. I decided to drop her off at the local emergency room. After I checked her in I told the nurse that I was going to the restroom. I left the hospital and drove home. I called the hospital to check on Sarah's condition. They would not give me any information about her. A few days later there was a headline in the local newspaper, "Young girl dropped off by mystery woman dies at Brunswick Emergency room." The article went on to say that a woman, matching my description, dropped a young girl off and she died a short time later. It went on to say that the police were looking for my make of car.

I feel so bad that I can't live with myself. I am starting to get very sleepy. I'd better hurry and address this to the local police department. I don't have much time left. I am truly sorry for what I did and I know Sarah has joined her mother in heaven and Mary will no longer be "A face in the window."

A MURDER AT
THE FRIENDSHIP

The Friendship Resort Hotel is located in Atlantic City, New Jersey. It had been in business for the last forty-three years. I have been going there every summer for a two week vacation for the past twenty years. It is normally the best place in New Jersey to experience peace and tranquility. For some reason the younger people have not adopted this area of New Jersey for their annual tear-up-the-hotel romps. Until this particular night, that is.

A rap on my door revealed two of New Jersey's finest. They wanted to know if I had heard any unusual noises the previous night. Like I said previously, it was normally pretty quiet around my hotel and its surrounding areas. I told the police that I was walking the beach most of the night and didn't return home until after midnight. They asked me if anyone saw me walking the beach and I told them no. I hope they don't think I had anything to do with those murders.

They told me that there had been two separate murders the previous night. Two separate murders! I was told by the police to remain at the hotel until they had interviewed everyone.

The manager of the hotel, Charlie Wenz, was a friend of mine. After all, I've been coming here for twenty years and I got to know him personally. I think I'll go to the office and see if he knows what's going on with these murders.

Charlie was a nervous wreck; he told me that the police were making a real pest out of themselves. He was especially worried about the reputation of the hotel. "Despite an outstanding level of security protocol, someone managed to murder two women", Charlie said. He was told by the police not to reveal any details of the murders, but he told me everything he knew.

He reported that, "Of the two women murdered late last night, one was twenty, and one was twenty-two years old. Both women were renting single rooms with single accommodation. It appears that both women were murdered in the same manner: strangulation. The appearance of their clothes indicated that both women were sexually violated. I overheard the medical examiner tell that to one of the policeman. The police had a few pieces of key evidence, two rags containing chloroform and some bloody sand. They told me they had a few suspects; a pair of bikers, a young bodybuilder, and two strange hitchhikers."

It was good the police never mentioned to Charlie about me being considered a suspect, or at least I thought they didn't tell him.

The police were a little puzzled; with all the security in place it appeared that both women opened their doors to someone they felt they could trust. There was no sign of forced entry in either of the rooms. They checked the alibis of all of their suspects; none had a record, but at the same time, none were squeaky clean.

While I was talking to Charlie, one of the policeman entered the office. He said, "Mr. Wenz, it looks like we're ready to wrap this case up.

New evidence has surfaced regarding the bloody sand and the chloroform, and a new suspect has emerged. It seems we overlooked someone: Joe, the handyman. He had been arrested for murder two years ago in Virginia Beach, Virginia and was released for lack of evidence. It seems Joe was a little. We found chloroform and bloody shoes hidden in his room."

Joe was arrested, and after a quick trial, he was sentenced to death in the New Jersey State Penitentiary. Joe still professes his innocence, and as he claimed in his trail, says he was set up by the real murderer.

Joe did not commit these murders; for you see—it was me. I planted the bloody sand and the bottle of chloroform in Joe's room when he was passed out from a night of heavy drinking. I think I'll return to Virginia Beach; there are plenty of resorts there and plenty of single women willing to trust a man of the cloth enough to open their doors to him.

A MURDER MYSTERY

THE BEGINNING - HOW IT STARTED

My name is Anne Hastings, and this is the sad story of my murder.

I'm thirty-three years old and was born and raised in Chicago, Illinois. I attended PS44 where I met my husband, Tom. We met at a school dance when we were both in tenth grade. I didn't think that couples met at dances anymore, but we did. They didn't have the internet or dating sites fifteen years ago, so I guess you could say that we met the old fashioned way.

On our first date, Tom took me to the local cinema. He was a complete gentleman and it didn't take me long to fall in love with him. I guess you could say it was love at first sight, another term not frequently used today. Tom showed no signs of aggression in the six years that we dated. Of course he lost his temper many times but his anger in any of those situations was never applied toward me.

After we were married things changed drastically. The anger that I said Tom had applied toward others was now almost always applied to me. For now Tom's anger was only verbal, not physical. I was afraid that it would lead to physical abuse, so I suggested to Tom that he see a therapist. He went ballistic on me and told me if I ever suggested that again I would be very sorry. He even went as far as telling me that I should see a therapist. Thank God I could have no children because I don't think I could find that a reason to stay with him.

Tom had a good job as a steamfitter and work was steady most of the time. I worked at a local office furniture dealer as a salesperson and my pay was mostly on commission. Tom and I rented a small house in a suburb outside of Chicago. If we were to split up, I knew I could manage the rent on my own and Tom would have no problem getting an apartment with his income.

I called my mom and told her that I was thinking of divorcing Tom. She suggested that I think it out and maybe give Tom another chance. She reminded me that she gave my father another chance when she found out that he was having an affair, and that they had thirty-five more years of a happy marriage. I lost my father a few years ago to cancer. He was a homicide detective with the Chicago Police department, and I'm sure he would know what I should do in my situation.

I called one of my father's old buddies, Sam Roth, and asked him if he had any ideas of what I should do. Sam asked me if Tom had ever gotten physical with me. I told him of the close calls that I had with him recently and that he refused to get any kind of help.

"All of the situations you have described advance to physical altercations," Sam said. He continued, "If you are serious about a divorce I suggest you get a peace bond against Tom immediately. I know an Alderman friend of mine who can draw one up for you. You will need to be there to sign the papers. The gentleman's name is Ross Green. and his office is located at 9th and Logan streets. I'll meet you there in two hours."

Mr. Green was very nice and he offered his sympathies on what I was going through. He said that peace bonds were the biggest part of his duties every week.

"What a shame," I thought.

Mr. Green went on, "What you're getting here Anne is a P.F.A., a protection from abuse, and from the way Sam had described your life with your husband, you're definitely going to need one. "I have a few more people coming to see me so Sam can tell you what to do now."

Sam asked me if I thought Tom knew him at all and I told him I didn't think so. Sam was retired but said he still had his police badge. He told me to gather up all of Tom's essential clothing and put them in a few nice boxes on the front porch and then telephone Tom where he is working and tell him about the bond.

Sam continued, "If he's anything like you described he will probably go nuts. Tell him that his clothes and toiletries will be in boxes on the front porch, and also tell him that I will be there to make sure everything goes smoothly."

Sam accompanied me to my house while I got Tom's things together. After I put the boxes out I called Tom as Sam had instructed. The job that Tom was working on was about a half hour drive from our place, but Tom pulled up in front of our house in twenty. When Sam saw how erratic Tom was driving he told me to step into the house and to stay inside no matter what Tom said to me.

Tom jumped out of his car screaming, "I

want to see that bitch! She can't throw me out of my own house!."

Sam flashed his badge while showing Tom the peace bond and said, "This form says she can, and as far as that goes, I know for a fact that you and Anne are only renting this house. Your wife is in the process of filing for a divorce, so I suggest you stay away from her until you are notified by mail to appear in court."

Tom said, "You can't protect her forever."

Sam said, "You better watch your ass, buster. I can take you down to the station and charged with attempted battery for threatening her."

Tom seemed to calm down a little. He took his boxes and said that he would be in touch with me about getting the rest of his stuff.

Sam said, "Look closely at that bond, Tom. You are to have no contact with your wife whether it be in person or via phone."

I thought, "Am I doing the right thing?"

THE BEGINNING
GETTING RID OF TOM

The next six months were pure torture. Tom would park outside of my office for hours at a time.

Sam said that there was nothing I could do about that because he wasn't actually talking or harassing me, or at least that's the way he said the police would see it. I received phone calls at all hours of night. When I picked up the phone, of course, he would hang up. I had to answer because my mother had a weak heart and I never knew if it was her calling or a hospital. One morning when

I went to put the key in my car's ignition I noticed a post it note stuck to the steering column that read, "Boom." Somehow Tom gained entrance to my car. I couldn't prove anything and had to suck it up, like they say.

I purchased movies from Amazon for viewing on my laptop because I was afraid to leave my house. I removed my name from all the social media sites I belonged to because Tom would somehow find my passwords for signing on these sites. Tom took quite a few computer courses before and after we were married. In fact he installed all the hardware on my laptop and was the one who trained me on its operation.

After our divorce was final, I thought things would change, but they remained pretty much the same. Tom never did find out that Sam wasn't a retired policeman. Sam saved me many times.

I made up my mind that I had to get out of Chicago and try to start a new life, but my mother's health was deteriorating and I thought if I moved it may kill her. Besides that, if I moved I would not be able to contact her. Tom was very sly and had the skills of a detective. I can't believe with this skill he never figured out that Sam wasn't on active duty, or maybe he did know all the time that he wasn't. I was beside myself and didn't know what to do.

My mother took care of my predicament – sadly, she died a few months after my divorce was final. Mom had her entire funeral paid for with her insurance, so I didn't have to bear that expense. I couldn't believe that louse came to the funeral home. I know he did it to spite me, because I could tell he disliked my mother from the first time he met her. I'm such an idiot. I should have dropped him right then.

I knew my dad had quite a few government bonds when he died, which were inherited by my mother upon his death. He was so old school. Everyone had CDs and he had U.S. government bonds. When my mother died I inherited those bonds, all ninety-five thousand dollars worth. Isn't it ironic that a bond kept Tom out of my life temporarily and now bonds will keep him out of my life forever? There was nothing to keep me in Chicago now, only a great aunt and a few cousins that never talked to me anyway. I did some research on cities and found out that in quite a few surveys, Pittsburgh, Pennsylvania was rated quite well. Well, Pittsburgh it was for me!

I thought I should sever all ties with Chicago, so I found a company that would buy all of the furniture that I owned. I donated most of my clothes and kept the clothes I would travel in and a few outfits to wear while I looked for a new job. I was assured by everyone that I dealt with, including my landlord, that they did not know where I had moved to. I didn't even tell Sam where I intended to go, or when. I decided to drive a rental car to Pittsburgh. I figured a plane, train, or bus would be too easy for Tom to trace me. I left my own car parked in front of my house and the lights on in my house. I figured if Tom saw this he'd think I may be on vacation or home sick, thus giving me more time to drive my rental to Pittsburgh.

A friend of mine I went to school with was a notary and I arranged to have my car title transferred to Sam. The car was a 2003 Chevy

Cobalt and was only worth three or four thousand dollars. I owed Sam that much at least. I sent the title and the keys to Sam's home with my intentions. I hoped he wouldn't be offended that I didn't tell him where I intended to move to. I trusted Sam, but there was no telling what Tom would do to find out where I was. Well, my journey to a new life began then.

MY MURDER - SETTLING IN

I hope I made the right choice when I chose Pittsburgh as my new home. I felt I had done enough research to make my decision. I was amazed at how many times I read that Pittsburgh had the friendliest people in the world. Any place would be friendlier than Chicago, Illinois. I know that Chicago is always getting a bad rap but I think in some ways it deserves it. And besides that, if I didn't get out of there when I did, Tom would have killed me for sure. It turns out he did anyway, but that will be covered a little later on.

I was fortunate to find a small house like I wanted so quickly. I'm glad I didn't have to use that much of my inheritance to pay for an extended motel stay. After leaving the motel, I would have to make my own bed and clean up after myself. I cleaned up after that slob for five years, so I should be able to clean up after myself with no trouble.

I know that all big cities have their share of drug problems – I just hope I made the right choice by settling in this Pittsburgh suburb, Trentview. I guess I should look into getting a dog for protection and companionship. I could have brought Duke with me but I preferred to sever all ties with that bastard Tom, including giving up my furry friend. The real estate agent said that this was an old neighborhood with a majority of retired seniors. I don't think I could listen to another blaring note of head-banger music coming from those gigantic car speakers. I have a few job interviews scheduled for the beginning of the week. I have to be very careful where I apply for employment. I'll need to work for a company who will be willing to keep any questions regarding my identity a secret. I obtained a letter from the Pittsburgh Police department, through Barney, describing my unique situation. With this letter any prospective company would receive limited information concerning my history from where I worked previously. They would be assured that they would never be in danger if they hired me. I hope the statement about any company being in danger is true because I think Tom can be very resourceful when it comes to locating me.

Most of the jobs I applied for were sales positions. I kept away from furniture sales because that's the first place Tom would check. I know that Chicago is far from Pittsburgh but Tom is a mean and vengeful person who would stop at nothing to locate and harm me.

Early one morning I received a call from a place I applied for employment at. It was a high end gift shop. I know the norm today is two or three interviews until you are possibly hired, but the personnel manager at this company, Mrs. Rossi, loved me. She read the copy of the letter from the Chicago Police Department and was familiar with my situation as she had a daughter who went through something like it. Sadly, her daughter met a horrible fate when her ex fatally shot her a few years after she was wed to him. I guess in that regard Pittsburgh was no different than Chicago when in came to domestic violence.

The name of my new employer was "A Needle in a Haystack." I don't know where or what that name has to do with gifts but it has worked for them for the past forty years. The company has over sixty locations in the United States and their big claim to fame is that all of their merchandise is manufactured in the United States. I was shocked to hear this. My working hours would be from 9 in the morning until 6 at night which included an hour for lunch. I was close to fast food restaurants and a few nicer restaurants. I will be able to take a trolley to work everyday and will be saving a great deal by not having a car for now and, if this works out, I may purchase a low mileage used automobile down the road.

MY MURDER - NEW NEIGHBORS

I think I'll go out to the front of the house and look around. Maybe one of those seniors will see me and decide to bake me cookies. You always see that in the movies, but I've never had anyone bake me cookies after moving into an old home.

There is an old couple down the street sitting on their porch. I say "old couple" to myself, but they're probably only in their sixties. Here I am at thirty-five hoping to reach thirty-six. Actually, as you read to the end of my story you'll realize that

I don't make it to my thirty-sixth birthday. I intend to mail this little story to the local authorities. There should be enough information to arrest and convict that bastard for first degree murder. I'm sorry; I'm supposed to be writing about my new neighbors, but my mind is so preoccupied with being murdered that it's hard to concentrate on anything else.

I'll try a friendly smile on the old couple. Hey she smiled back, but he gave me the most rotten look I have seen in a long time. Oh no, he's getting up and coming towards me. What do I do now? It's too late because here he is. He said, "I hope you don't blare any of that Rap junk on your radio. My wife and I both go to bed early and we tend to sleep in late, sometimes damn near six or seven in the morning."

You would think by my first interaction with this old guy that he was mean or ornery. I don't think that was the case here. I think the old gentleman was trying to act tough and I could tell from looking at him that he didn't have a mean bone in his body.

My thoughts were confirmed when the gentleman's wife said, "Quit trying to scare that young lady, you old fart. Bring her over here so we can meet her." After he brought me over, she introduced herself. "Hello Sweetie, my name is Gladys Jones, and this old coot is Big Barney. I know he doesn't look that big to you, but he's bigger than Barney who lives across the street from you. My Barney is always barking orders or complaints at people. He thinks he's still a homicide detective."

I got to know Gladys and Barney very well and confided with them all my secrets about why I left Chicago and decided to settle in Pittsburgh. I told them about the verbal abuse and near beatings I endured under my ex-husband, Tom. Barney understood what I was talking about a little more than Gladys because he saw it many times while working for the force in Pittsburgh. I felt bad not getting to know my other neighbors, but with my situation, the fewer people that knew me the better off I would be, or so I thought.

MY MURDER - PROTECTION

I decided I was going to need a gun for my protection. I found a local gun dealer who also offered instructions on how to fire and maintain one. I told the dealer about my circumstance. He sympathized with me and suggested a Luger P08, a light hand gun recommended for women. The dealer helped with all of the paperwork, the waiting period, and everything I needed to know about the weapon. I completed my training and wouldn't quite call myself a sharpshooter, but I qualified in firing the Luger.

ALL SET

Well I felt I was ready to take a shot at my new life. I have a job, a house, neighbors who care about me and protection if I'm threatened by Tom, or anyone else. Or again, so I thought.

THE ACTUAL MURDER

I was lying in bed watching David Letterman when I thought I heard a noise downstairs. I turned the television off and my suspicions were confirmed. There was definitely someone or something down there. I reached in my night stand for my Luger, and remembered that I had left it on the kitchen table in pieces. I intended to clean it but got tired and changed my mind. I thought to myself, "The first thing to do is call 911." Do you believe I left my cell phone on the kitchen table beside my gun? Everyone told me I didn't need a landline phone since a cell phone would be sufficient.

I better make a decision quickly because I think it has to be Tom. I reached in the nightstand and retrieved my large pair of sewing scissors. That's the only weapon I could think of in my room. I thought of screaming but I doubt anyone would hear me or bother to do anything about it. The only one that might worry about me would be Barney or Gladys, but they lived too far down the street to hear me. I guess I should have gotten a little closer with my other neighbors, but the fewer people who know me, the better my chances of Tom finding out where I was hiding.

I turned the TV back on with the volume very low and tried to make my bed look like I was sleeping in it. I positioned myself around the little corner from my door. I figured if he entered with his gun first, my plan was to stab him in the hand with my scissors. After that I planned on running for my life. My legs were shaking so bad that I was hoped I wouldn't give my position away. As the door slowly opened, two shots rang out. I was startled and opened the door all the way. Another shot rang out and I felt a burning sensation in my chest. I looked to see if Tom was dead, but it wasn't Tom on the floor. It was someone I have never seen before in my life. I looked down at him, and heard a voice say, "Do you know who this guy is?" It was Barney speaking to me, standing there with a smoking gun in his hand. It turns out that my next door neighbor saw someone milling around my house and she knew that Barney was a retired detective, so she called him and told him what was going on. Barney knew my situation and immediately came to my house armed and ready.

Barney looked at me and said, "My God, young lady, you've been shot!" In all the confusion, believe it or not, I actually forgot about the pain in my chest, until I saw all the blood on my nightgown and on the floor.

Barney told me that he called 911 before he came over to my house. He checked the pulse of the guy on the floor and said, "He's a'goner. I guess I still have it. Two hits to the head."

"Yeah, Barney, but there were three shots."

"He must've got one off that hit you."

I found out later in the hospital that the third shot was from Barney's gun. I guess he still didn't have it quite as he thought he did. My prognosis is good and I'm in guarded condition right now. Thank God I wasn't hit with that third shot from Barney's gun a little lower or I wouldn't be writing this now.

THE INVESTIGATION

Sergeant Jakes apologized for seeing me so soon after my hallowing experience. He said that it was always a good idea to interview the victim, while pertinent details were still fresh in their mind. The sergeant told me I could call him Jim if I felt more comfortable. I agreed.

Jim said, "I would also like to apologize for Barney's poor marksmanship, but if it wasn't for him coming to your house and calling 911, you would probably be in the morgue right now. We obtained the identity of your assailant with the help of your Father's friend, Sam Roth. Sam also hooked us up with Alderman Ross Green, the man who issued the peace bond against your ex-husband, Tom. He filled us in on a lot of your history. Getting back to your assailant, his name was, Ed Cummings, a small time hood from the Chicago area. His jacket contained numerous burglaries and assaults, but never a murder attempt. I guess someone paid him a pretty penny to murder you, and I'm guessing that someone would be your ex-husband, Tom. We don't have any proof yet, but I intend to work closely with the Chicago Police Department to find out exactly who hired this Cummings guy in his attempt to murder you. From my communications so far with Chicago, there has been no sign of your ex-husband anywhere. I understand that you will be released in a few days, so we want to provide you as much protection as you need to avoid something like this happening again. Let's not forget that if your ex is involved, he may make an attempt on your life again. I understand that you own a firearm and know how to use it. I suggest this time that you keep it near by at all times or at least until we capture who is trying to harm you."

After ten days in the hospital I was released. As soon as I arrived home I called a locksmith that Barney had suggested a few weeks earlier. I wanted to have new deadbolt locks installed on the front and rear doors. I saw a special on the local TV station on home security and it showed how easily burglars could access your home through inferior deadbolt locks. I checked my doors and saw that they were the ones that were shown to be easily accessible. The newer ones I had installed were much more secure.

BACK TO WORK

After a few weeks of physical therapy and a few weeks of rest and relaxation, I was ready to return to work. Mrs. Rossi welcomed me with opened arms. She cried when she first saw me and seemed emotionally drained. I think she was reliving the horrors of her daughter's murder.

It took a while to get back in my old routine, but eventually I got used to it again. I had trouble going to sleep at night. I kept imagining sounds coming from my first floor. I guess it will take a while until I can sleep through the night without being afraid. I could buy a sleeping aid at the local pharmacy, but any of those medications may make me sleep too soundly and I would never hear a potential intruder. I wonder what horrible thing I did in my life to deserve to live in this constant fear.

THE END OF MY LIFE

For some reason I'm really feeling queasy tonight. It's almost time for Letterman, so I think I'll turn in. I have my pistol and my phone with me, so I'm prepared for almost anything. On my way up my stairs there was a knock on my door. Who could it be this late at night? I thought to myself, "I don't think an intruder would knock."

When I looked through the glass on my front door I saw my neighbor, Barney. I immediately opened the door and said, "What's up Barney, and why are you here so late at night?"

Barney said, "Gladys just woke me up and said she thought she saw someone creeping around the front of your house. That woman has eyes like a hawk. I thought I better check it out. I see you have your cell phone with you, but where is your pistol?"

I purchased a leg pistol holster recently and I showed Barney where the pistol was.

"Is that a Luger P08 you have there, Bernie asked me?"

I said, "Yes it is, Barney," as I took it out of the leg holster to show it to him.

Barney said, "This is an excellent piece for a woman. Light, but powerful."

Suddenly Barney was standing in front of me with my Luger pointing at me. I said, "What the hell are you doing, Barney?"

Barney said, "I really like you sweetie, but your ex-husband made me an offer I couldn't refuse. He really must want you dead. Do you know what the City of Pittsburgh pays me as a pension? Oh hell, I don't think you're too interested in that now. I'm going to tell you how this is going to play out. You're going to walk up those steps and commit suicide in your bedroom. Everyone knows that you are frightened with the world you are living in and you just had enough. When the police rule your death a suicide, it will release your ex from any guilt. That way everyone wins, except you, unfortunately."

I pleaded with Barney to forget his gruesome plan, and even assured him that I would not tell a soul about what happened here. Of course I was lying, and I assume Barney knew that I was.

"Okay kiddo, let's go upstairs," he said. "Let's not make this difficult. I could kill you right here and drag you up the stairs, but that is not my plan. So, it's your choice, die here, or live a few more minutes and die upstairs in your room."

I said, "I'd prefer to live a few extra minutes."

As we approached the top step I looked back and noticed that Barney was carrying my pistol facing skyward like they do on TV when they enter a room. Thank God for me Barney's old police days were still with him. I calked my leg and kicked him in the chest, while holding onto the railing. Barney tried to grab the railing but it was out of his reach. He tumbled down the steps, and then there was an eerie silence. I hoped that he had broken his neck or was at least unconscious from the fall. I wasn't taking any chances by checking to see which fate he succumbed to. My cell and my pistol were still with or near him. I ran up to my room and crawled out on the second floor roof and began to scream my lungs out. I saw lights go on in a few houses, and then the man across the street asked me if I was alright. He told me that his wife had called 911 and that the police were on their way. My neighbor told me he was getting his ladder to let me off the roof. We agreed we should keep away from my downstairs.

It seemed like a lifetime, but the police arrived in probably three or four minutes. I told them what had happened and they entered my house with their guns drawn. By then there was a huge crowd of neighbors standing behind a police rope-off. These were the neighbors that I refused to get to know. One woman brought me a terry cloth robe to wear. It's a shame that the world we live in today is so unfriendly. No one wants to get to know their neighbors. Years ago we knew everyone on our block and always left the front and back doors open. Those days are far behind us.

About a half hour later two ambulances arrived, one for me, and one for Barney. It appears that he was only knocked out from the fall. I was hoping that he was dead, and then I thought that by him being alive was a much better scenario for me. Hopefully he can testify at trial that my ex-husband had paid to have me murdered.

EPILOGUE

After a lengthy trail Barney was sentenced to ten to twenty years for attempted murder. He made a deal with the DA by testifying against my ex; I can't call him by name anymore. Barney could have received a twenty to life sentence.

Maybe he'll live long enough to return to his wife in Pittsburgh. I couldn't care less either way.

My ex drew a female judge for his murder trial. She was sympathetic towards women and the way that some of them had been treated. My ex was sentenced to life with no chance of parole. The judge said that she wanted to make sure that I would never be threatened by that man again.

I couldn't find myself living in Pittsburgh anymore. I liked the city, but couldn't live near Barney's wife and seeing her every day. Besides that, she thought Barney was an innocent, poor soul. I moved back to Chicago, picked up the pieces of my life, and started to live a fear free life. I moved into a nice neighborhood in the suburbs and immediately introduced myself to my neighbors.

For you readers who were expecting my murder, I'm sorry to disappoint you, but you should know by now, "No one likes an unhappy ending."

A SUICIDE AT ST. LUKE'S

It was 5:30 AM on a Tuesday morning and I entered St. Luke's to prepare the church for 6am mass. I had to turn all the necessary lights on, prepare my vestments for the mass, and make sure that the church was prepared.

My name is Father John, and I've been the pastor at St. Luke's in downtown Detroit, Michigan, for the past thirty years. Thirty years ago, the 6am mass had probably a hundred parishioners in attendance. In fact, we had two masses thirty years ago, a 6am and an 8am. If we're lucky today there will be fifteen in attendance. Ours is an old church with mostly parishioners of Italian background, and they prefer the 6am over the 8am, so with the lack of attendance over the years the 8am mass was eliminated.

As I flicked the main floor light switch on I noticed someone sitting in the front pew. How could this be and how did they enter the church? I cautiously called out to whoever it was and received no reply. As I got closer to the person I recognized who it was; it was Kim Jackson, a local woman who I had counseled frequently. Kim was a drug addict and a prostitute. I called out Kim's name again and then noticed some kind of wound on her head. I felt for Kim's pulse, although I've seen enough crime shows to know that Kim was most likely dead. I didn't detect a pulse, so I immediately called 911 and reported the incident.

Right at that time, Joe Facetti entered

the church. Joe was a devout Catholic and an all-around church helper. Joe was the first to get to mass and always available for small repairs that needed done in our old building. He was also very financially generous with St. Luke's as well.

As Joe approached me, he spotted Kim. He said, "Oh my God, Father, what has happened here?" I told Joe that I had just arrived myself, and that I had called 911.

Joe said, "I noticed the front basement window was ajar, and I was going to tell you about it, but this probably has something to do with that. I won't repair it until the authorities have come."

I thanked Joe and asked him if he would go in the sacristy and find some materials to make a sign before any other parishioners came in. I told Joe to make a small sign telling parishioners that the church would be closed until the following morning until we had some emergency plumbing repairs taken care of—I didn't want to create a panic by telling them what I discovered. I swore Joe to secrecy on the matter.

After Joe left I decided I'd check out the crime scene a little closer. On the floor was a small caliber revolver. I've seen enough TV to know that I should not touch anything, and risk compromising the crime scene.

About a week after the incident I received a call from the police department. They told me that Kim's death was ruled a suicide. That was no surprise to me, but asking me to come down to the station did.

I arrived at the station soon after I was called and was directed to Sgt. Boone, the investigator in charge of the case. He greeted me and told me he had information for me concerning the case. He handed me a crumpled piece of paper and said, "I'll need this for evidence but I think you should read it. After all, it is addressed to you.

It read: "Dear Father John. I am sorry that I took my life, and I'm sorry for the life that I led. I can't continue the life that I was leading without putting people's lives in danger. Please pray to God for me and ask for my forgiveness. Kim."

Sgt. Boone said, "There was a medical form also found in Miss Jackson's purse. It's from Mercy Hospital and it appears that she was in the final stage of AIDS and did not have long to live. I know you knew Miss Jackson and I'm sorry for your loss."

I went back to St. Luke's to pray to God for Kim's forgiveness and asked Him to welcome her to His house.

GOD'S SOLUTION

Betty and I have been married for almost fifty-five years now. The only time we were apart was during my four year stint in the Coast Guard. We were physically apart, but connected through our hearts and our minds. I telephoned when I could and wrote a letter every day, to my love. Sometimes it was just a short note, but at least it was something.

Together we raised three boys and two girls. They have successful careers, and we are very proud of them. Our grandchildren are an extension of their lives, and I thank God everyday for sending them to Betty and I.

With my Coast Guard pension, my other from working at Sears, and Betty's state pension from teaching, I'd say we are pretty well off financially. Everything seemed to be coasting along fine, until we received a call from our family physician. Something showed up on one of Betty's routine tests. We had completed our yearly physicals a couple weeks before the call. It's funny—I'm the one with multiple medical problems and Betty had never been sick a day in her life. I can't remember the last time she visited a doctor for any problems.

We knew we had to face this situation, and we knew we were going to do it together. We decided to let our faith in God be our driving force in dealing with this. I'm hoping that we are not shooting the gun, as they say, since we haven't even seen our doctor yet. We decided to keep the children out of this until we knew something more.

225

We arrived at our doctor's office with a very positive state of mind, but that was short lived. It appears that Betty may have brain cancer. Our doctor told us that he had consulted with a few doctors specializing in the field and said we had better see a specialist as soon as possible, because the type of cancer that Betty may have could be very fast spreading and should be acted upon on quickly. We made an appointment for the following week for a specialist that our doctor recommended and hoped for the best.

After more tests than you can imagine, we had a consultation scheduled. I hope this doctor doesn't play poker with his fellow physicians. From the look on his face we could tell that the news would not be good.

The doctor informed us that he had diagnosed Betty with inoperable brain cancer. He asked Betty if she had experienced any pain in her head. She said she had, but she attributed it to the chronic migraine headaches she had experienced for the last five years. The doctor surmised that the head pains Betty started receiving approximately five years earlier was the start of the cancer and not migraine headaches.

We consulted with the children now that we know what the problem seemed to be. As a family we decided to get two more opinions. We trusted our doctor, but when you're dealing with your life, all options should be looked at. Unfortunately the other two opinions were the same. So we went back to our cancer specialist and asked him what would be the best action to take at that point in time. The doctor said he would schedule treatments for

Betty, but that the treatments would only relieve the pain somewhat and were in no way a cure.

The treatments were doing no good and Betty was suffering excruciating pain constantly. If she slept two hours in a day, it was a lot.

One night Betty asked me if I loved her. I was shocked that she would even ask me a question like that. I replied, "Of course I do, my dear. You are my life."

Betty looked at me and said, "I want you to end my life. I am in so much pain, believe me, I no longer want to live. I'm sure God will understand. This is something I want you to do because I don't have the nerve to do it myself. I will write a note explaining that I wanted you to do this thing. Believe me, you are too old to be sent to prison. Please Ed, please do this for me." I was in shock. This was a morbid request from the love of my life that I would never, ever entertain.

Betty continued. She said, "I know you have a 22 starter pistol in the garage. That should be a sufficient tool to end my painful life. I have one more important request for you my love. I don't want to know when this is going to happen. Also, please do not discuss this with any of the children since they may try to talk you out of it." I told Betty that I would think about her morbid request, and I kissed her good-night.

Betty and I were members of St. Catherine's church in our community. I called Father John and asked if I could meet with him as soon as possible. He told me, of course, and that he would be waiting for me.

I explained everything to Father John. "Your

227

wife is in so much pain and probably has trouble reasoning at this time, otherwise she would never ask you to something of that nature. I will pray for you and Betty. I suggest that you stay in church for a while and ask God for guidance in this matter. I'm sure he will provide a solution."

I stayed in church for approximately two hours asking God for guidance.

When I arrived home and walked into our bedroom, I knew that my dear love had passed. She had a smile on her face and she looked so happy. It looked as though all the pain had left her body. I noticed a note beside the phone on our nightstand. It read:

"Sweetheart, I am sorry for what I asked you to do. I prayed with all of my heart for God to take my life, releasing that burden from you. As you read this note I know that God has answered my prayers, as well as yours."

Your loving and grateful wife, Betty.

GUILTY OR INNOCENT?

How did I get into this mess? Tomorrow, eight women and four men will begin the trial process to determine if I am guilty or innocent for the brutal murder of my wife. My attorney assured me my chances for acquittal were very good as the prosecution's evidence was all circumstantial.

I was twenty years younger than my wife, Jean. It was not love at first sight. Jean was my secretary for ten years and we got along as boss and employer for those ten years. But as soon as I divorced my first wife, Rita, Jean seemed to have a different interest in me – a romantic one. I welcomed this interest willingly, because my first wife had become cold and distant towards me in the last couple years of our marriage.

When Jean and I married, we acted like teenagers at first, holding hands and looking into each others eyes lovingly every waking minute of the day. This scenario lasted for a few years and then I felt that she was becoming distant. I noticed strange e-mail names on her laptop. We had an agreement that we would never look at each others e-mail messages, but when Jean's behavior became erratic, I thought I'd glance at her computer and see if anything looked out of the ordinary. At first I merely looked at the sender's names, but when I noticed a frequency in seeing one particular name, I decided to open one of the messages. It appears that Jean and this fellow, Saul, had been seeing each other for over two years. We were only married for four years, so this affair must have started a couple of years after we were married. Everyone tried to tell me that Jean was only after my money, which is why I suggested we have a prenuptial agreement. Jean willingly signed the pre-nup, and this set my mind at ease. But now I'm guessing that she is screwing around with this Saul guy because of that agreement. Maybe he has a lot of money like I do.

The night of the grizzly murder, I went to a local theater by myself. I said nothing to Jean about my discoveries on her computer. She and I preferred different kinds of movies, so I frequently went by myself. Jean told me that she was going clothes shopping at a local mall. Lord knows, she could use more clothes. She was probably going to meet that loser, Saul.

I returned home from the theater around nine o'clock. Jean's car was in the driveway. Maybe she actually did do some shopping. I opened the rear door leading to our kitchen and made a gruesome discovery. Jean was lying on the kitchen floor in a large pool of blood. In fact there was blood splattered everywhere. No matter how hard I try, I can't get that image out of my mind. Beside Jean's body was a huge butcher knife, the kind used to carve ham or turkeys. Like a fool I picked it up to see if it was our knife. Of course it was our kitchen butcher knife. no one would bring their own butcher knife to a murder and just leave it there. I tried to wipe my finger prints off the knife but I figured that it would look bad to the police so I laid it back down where I found it and called 911 to report the murder.

The police arrived about fifty minutes later with the coroner and a forensic team. It must have been a slow night for murders for them to show up that quickly. I gave the police my preliminary statement and I could tell that the detective who questioned me didn't believe me.

I was taken down to police headquarters and was questioned again by a different detective. I gave him the same story as I gave the detective who questioned me at my house. I could tell that this guy didn't believe me either. The fact that I didn't go anywhere else where someone could have recognized me didn't help.

The detective who interviewed me at the precinct mentioned the age difference between my wife and I. I asked him what that had to do with anything and he told me not to worry about it, and that he was the one asking the questions. He asked if I had a place to stay because my home would be taped off for about a week while evidence was being gathered. He also mentioned that an autopsy would need to be performed. I told him I would stay with my grandson, SG. I was surprised when his father called him that, and I was surprised when he showed up at the station and offered to put me up until I could get back into my home. I was never that close to he or his father. Maybe he was another vulture looking to inherit some of my money.

About a week later I was called to the precinct again. The same detective asked me if I knew my wife was pregnant. I said that was impossible because I had a vasectomy performed around four years ago.

He looked at me and said, "My friend, you have just supplied us with a motive in your wife's murder. We're assuming that your wife approached you and revealed her pregnancy and you killed her in a jealous rage. There was a lot of anger involved in this killing and something like that could trigger it. This, plus the fact that I checked and found out that you have a record for domestic violence adds credence to my assumption."

I told him that I was accused of this charge by my first wife, Rita, not Jean.

He said it didn't matter who accused me because I was still charged with domestic violence, and was found guilty, fined, and received probation. I was booked on a general charge of first degree homicide and housed in the local jail. At a hearing a few days later, I was granted bail based on the fact I wasn't considered a flight risk and of my excellent standing in the local community.

A few incriminating facts came up at my murder trial, which lasted only two weeks. My ex-wife, Rita, testified against me in regards to the domestic violence charge. She said, "He often threatened to stab me, but the night he grabbed a knife from the kitchen drawer I called 911 and the police came and arrested him. I believed he was going to kill me that night."

I really didn't want the jury to hear that. Also, Jean's doctor testified that I had approached him and asked she was being treated for. Of course he said he was not permitted to disclose any medical information about my wife to him. I hoped the jury wouldn't think that somehow I knew about my wife's pregnancy, which would not look good.

The e-mails from my wife's mystery lover, Saul, never came up at the trial. My lawyer told me that if this information was revealed to the jury, they may assume that I did kill her in a jealous rage. My lawyer assured me that I had a good chance for acquittal because he had done a great job in my defense. He said that there was a motive, but it was never clearly established, and that there was no incriminating evidence against me as all the evidence was purely circumstantial.

I believed in our judicial system and felt strongly I would be set free. When your life is hanging in the balance, you count on the integrity of your jury, and I was counting on mine. I believe that there was not enough evidence that I murdered my wife and I was hoping my jury felt the same way.

After twelve long hours of deliberation, the jury was ready with their verdict. The judge asked the foreman if the jury had arrived at a unanimous decision. The foreman said, "We have, your honor. We find the defendant innocent of all charges."

I think my lawyer and I were the only happy ones in that courtroom. You could hear the sounds of disgust coming from the gallery.

As I think about the whole experience the word, "Double jeopardy," comes to mind. I was tried and found not guilty, and can never be charged with this crime again. I'll miss my cheating wife and I'll never forgive her for what she did to me. If I had a chance I'd probably kill her again and hope for another sympathetic jury.

A couple of weeks after the trial I received a

letter from my grandson, SG. I had been meaning to call him and thank him for putting me up for that week, and for attending the trial every day. He was the only one on my side of the family who attended, since not even my own son made an appearance. I opened the letter and it contained a congratulations card on being found innocent in my murder trial. Boy, they make cards for any occasion or situation today. As I read the printed signature on the card I felt a slight pain in my chest. The printed signature was, "Saul Gregory Green, (SG)."

I DIDN'T DESERVE THIS

I was married to Judy for fifteen years. We had a combative marriage, which was equally the fault of both of us. I spent many a night in the local lock-up for smacking Judy around. Why is it that the husband is always the one to spend the night in jail when most of the fights were instigated by their wives? I drank entirely too much and Judy was always looking for the ultimate high. She experimented with every drug known to man. I could say that I drank because of her drug habit, but the more I think about it I had a drinking problem before we ever met. Judy eventually died of a massive stoke which the doctors attributed to her drug abuse. She was only forty-two years old.

Judy's parents hated me from the first time they met me. They thought I wasn't good enough for their precious daughter, and they were probably right. After Judy died her parents severed all ties with me, but now they had to see me for the reading of her will. Judy's parents were quite wealthy and often showered her with expensive gifts, as well as monetary ones.

After Judy died, I drank more than ever. This overindulgence led to me rob a local bank. I must have really been loaded, because I never would have robbed a bank knowing that I had all that cash coming from Judy's will. Maryland state law says that the spouse gets all of the other spouse's possessions, but Judy's parents were constantly trying to prove that I was incapable of controlling her estate. Judy's parents had run out of options and I had to travel across state to see what my little sweetie had left me to spend frivolously.

I was convicted of the robbery charge and am currently out on bail. I can travel to the will reading because it fits to my bail agreement.

I got a late start and the weather forecasters were calling for severe thunderstorms. My car had an illegal inspection so I had to travel at night and via back roads. There was a light drizzle when I departed, but the closer I got to my destination the harder the rains came. And then the thunderstorms started. It was just my luck that the weatherman was correct, for a change. I guess I shouldn't have drank so much before I started on this little excursion, because I was beginning to get sleepy. I hope there's a motel on this road so I can get a little shut eye.

Well my bad luck turned into good luck. There was a motel in my sights, and even through the heavy rains I could make out a vacancy sign. As I pulled up to the office, I noticed that the motel was painted the brightest shade of red I've ever seen in my life. On the side of the office was a classic Cadillac automobile, which looked like it was painted the same bright red as the motel. The outside grounds looked as though they were well taken care of, so I assumed the rooms would be taken care as well. It was two o'clock in the morning and I hoped someone would answer my knock on their door.

A very large older gentleman answered the door. He introduced himself as Lou Cifer and said that he had managed the motel for longer than he could remember. I apologized for stopping so late in the evening, but after I explained my circumstances he said that there was no bother. Lou told me that all the other rooms were occupied but he had room 666 still available. I thought to myself, "666 is a strange number for a motel with one floor." I observed that there were no other cars parked in the lot even though Lou said that all of the rooms were occupied except room 666. I blew these things off because I was dead on my feet and I needed to rest my eyes for an hour or two.

Lou was about to open the door to the room when for some strange reason I started thinking about Judy. I realized that she was the best thing that ever happened to me, despite her drug problems. I finally felt sorry that I had abused my wife the way that I did. "That's all water over the dam, maybe I'll treat my next wife a little better," I thought to myself.

Lou said, "Are you ready to see your room?"

I don't know why, but I had this feeling of impending doom. As I entered the room I felt my death was near. There was a very bright light ahead of me. I thought, "Oh my God, I'm dead and entering Heaven."

Just then I heard Judy's voice and saw her image in the bright light. She said, "Hello Dick, I've prepared this room especially for you."

I turned to thank Lou for his hospitality but he was gone, and so was the door. Judy's image disappeared and immediately flames started shooting from the floor. It was hotter than Hell. Metal bars suddenly formed on the walls as I began to melt in my custom fiery cell. My body was gone, but my soul remained. I had no idea a soul could burn in this flaming home for eternity. I was not going to be a guest of God, but a guest of the Devil's apostle, Lou Cifer.

JUSTIFIABLE HOMICIDE

I'm married to a man who is a real slob. I can't count the times over the last ten years I caught him cheating on me. He beat me and our children as well. I've called the police numerous times but at the last moment I refused to testify on him. I think it was a combination of me being scared of him and being left to fend for myself and the kids if he went to jail. He has a decent job and makes decent money. I have no skills, having married right out of high school. I was always meaning to get my GED but it seems like I never had enough time to get it.

A divorce was out of the question. He had mentioned numerous times that if I ever filed for one, he would kill me, and I believed him.

I had to come up with a plan to get that scum out of my life. He came home every night drunk and hardly ever took a bath. These two factors may contribute to my plan to put that waste in an early grave. The fact that he liked oldies was another factor in my murderous scheme.

I had to think of a good reason why he should take a bath. It was hard explaining anything to this jerk because of the inebriated condition he was in most of the time, but I gave it my best shot. I told him I received a phone call for him, and a lawyer told me that he had inherited some money and that he wanted to see him the next day to sign some papers. I think he grasped at what I had said to him. I told him that his appointment was for 1:00 the next afternoon, and I suggested that he take his bath in the morning. He mumbled some obscenities at me, but agreed.

I suppose because he had the day off, he started to drink the first thing after he got up. He was pretty sloshed by 10. I set our old console radio up beside the tub and set the dial to his oldies station. I waited until I heard the water sloshing around, and then I entered the bathroom with a smile on my face. He looked up at me and I said, "Goodbye." I pushed the electric radio into his tub of water and watched as he screamed and crackled all over the place. When I was sure he was dead I pulled the plug out of the outlet.

I dialed 911 and reported an accident at my house. The operator told me that my husband was probably dead but an ambulance would be dispatched to my house immediately.

After a week of investigating I was informed by the DA's office that my husband's death was ruled an accident. I had a nice juicy insurance policy on him with a double payment due in case of an accidental death. I met with an agent and was told that after their conversation with the authorities they ascertained that my husband's death was an accident, and payment would be sent by registered mail to me within 30 days.

About a week later, I received another visit from the local authorities. One of them had a huge brown envelope in his hand. He looked at me and said, "Do you know what this is, Mam?" It appears your husband feared for his life and suspected you may try to murder him. He knew about the accident clause and wrote a letter detailing your drinking habits, your constant infidelity, and your abuse of him and your children. It appears that he was not as stupid as I thought he was. It appears that I was the stupid one. I denied all of those accusations but after hours of interrogation I admitted to them that I killed my husband.

After a trial that lasted nine weeks I was convicted of first degree murder and sentenced to life plus twenty years. It appears the jury didn't believe my self-defense plea. It also appears that the jury believed all of the derogatory remarks about me. To add insult to injury it was overheard by one jury member, "We're surprised he didn't try to kill her!"

THE MYSTERY FLIGHT

After a long fight with cancer, my wife of forty years passed away. We received the customary three opinions, but the diagnosis was always the same: inoperative ovarian cancer.

Jeanie believed in the hereafter. The closer she got to death the more she talked about it. She frequently told me, "I am going to another time and I will make sure you are there too."

I entertained her fantasy. I knew all the drugs she was taking were surely affecting her mind and reasoning. When she talked about her hereafter it seemed to perk her up, and it helped her pass the time.

Jeanie wanted to die in our home. Near the end she had hospice nurses attending her needs every day. We still had our nights and we would reminisce and speak of our lives together.

I was not a completely faithful husband. In our forty years of marriage I had six affairs. I thought about confessing to Jeanie, but figured there wouldn't be any point in it. I could see no reason for her to take those facts with her. I was discreet in my affairs, and Jeanie had no idea I had ever been unfaithful. At least I thought as much.

The hospice nurse told me it was a matter of days until my Jeanie's death. While talking to her that night, she could tell I had heard some disturbing news. She made me promise when I knew her death was near that I would tell her.

That night she said, "You remember your promise, don't you? How much time do I have?"

"The nurse said a month at the most," I said.

Jeanie told me she had been thinking about her hereafter more and more and said she knew of a way that I could also go. "I've come up with a phrase for you to look for. The phrase will be: Jeanie's calling, and she's ready Jack."

I continued to amuse her and said, "Yes my dear, I will be looking for that phrase."

Jeanie passed away ten days later. I had as beautiful a funeral as I could for her. It was hard to believe she was gone. I casually thought to myself, "Well, I guess I better start looking for that phrase."

It had been a couple days since my Jeanie died. I thought I'd check to see if I'd received any mail. The mail typically seemed to be junk mail and various bills. But there it was, a letter addressed to me in my wife's handwriting, and there was no postmark on the letter. I told no one of Jeanie's delusions, so I was puzzled. Who could have placed this letter in my mail box? I started to shake all over. Was Jeanie's plan becoming a reality? I cautiously opened the letter and there it was in large printed red letters, "Jeanie's calling, and she's ready Jack." I almost passed out, feverishly grasping for air. I was shaking so much I was dangerously close to falling out of the chair. I thought to myself, "Maybe this is a bad dream, but it seemed so real." In the letter was an airline ticket and an additional sheet of paper with instructions for me. The destination on the ticket read, "Unknown." The additional sheet of paper was also in Jeanie's handwriting and read, "I know you are shocked Jack, but you must follow my instructions 'To the T' for this to work."

I didn't know what to do so I decided to get my affairs in order, just in case I wasn't coming back. I thought to myself, "What are you getting yourself into, Jack? You should just burn this letter and get on with your life." But then a crazy thought entered my mind, "Maybe this is for real. I'm getting up in years and there aren't many left. Maybe I'll take a shot at this."

Jeanie's instructions said to bring no luggage. I drove to the airport, anticipating my trip. Don't ask me why, but I parked in the short-term lot. I went directly to the list of departing flights after entering the airport. On the schedule was a departure listed as "Unknown," and the flight was to depart in only a few minutes, so I knew I'd better get moving. There was a plane on the runway with huge writing on the side of it. It read, "Jeanie's calling, and she's ready Jack." This seemed to be getting more real every minute.

I arrived at the departure gate where a female attendant was standing. "Oh, so you're Jack. Jeanie is waiting for you."

She had a devilish grin on her face while she spoke to me. In fact, if you'd put a set of horns on her head, she could have passed for the devil himself. I walked up the steps to the cabin and entered. When I arrived in the cabin, I began to perspire profusely and wondered if I was having a heart attack. I felt an extraordinary amount of heat and a colossal wall of fire. I thought, "What the hell is going on? Is this my wife's gift to me for all my indiscretions?" Just then, a deep gravely voice found its way through the fire. It said, "You should have resisted your adulteress desires."

I tried desperately to wake up. All of this had to be a bad dream. I prayed to God, "Please let me wake up". I woke up and realized that I was definitely having a nightmare, but where was all this heat coming from? I quickly realized I had been smoking in bed again and that the bedroom was on fire. I desperately tried to get out of my bed, but the intense fire was beginning to consume me. I heard sirens and women screaming outside my window. I realized then that I wasn't in my bedroom. I was in another place. I realized the women screaming were not outside my house, but were in the room with me. Through the fire I recognized them. They were the women I had my affairs with. They were screaming from the intense heat. I finally accepted the fact that this was not a dream, and that I would spend all of eternity in this hell.

I recalled what Jeanie said to me, "I am going to another time, and I will make sure that you are in that time." Ironically I was in that time with Jeanie, but I wasn't in the same place.

THE KID FROM ELDORADO

He was a scrawny 19-year old kid who could draw his gun with lightning speed. Clem's Ma' told him that a fast gun would not help him to complete any chores that she had assigned him to do, especially gathering stray steeds.

Clem's parents owned a horse farm on the outskirts of Eldorado, Texas. The farm was small, but horses from the farm were considered the finest in the West. Clem's Pa', Elmer, was always looking for Clem to help on the farm, but he could rarely be found. He was always somewhere practicing his fast draw.

Clem's favorite practicing spot was in front of an old faded mirror that he set up in an abandoned farm about three miles from his property. I say "his" property because his father told him that because he was the only son, he would leave the property to Clem when he couldn't care for it anymore.

When Clem practiced, he would picture himself the victor, while smiling into the mirror at his opponent's demise. He decided he should practice his draw outside in the morning, because any gunfight he ever witnessed was performed in the early hours. He would start practicing the next week because he had a load of chores to do for his Pa' now.

Clem went to town for supplies once a week with his Pa'. He spent what little free time he had telling everyone that he was the fastest gun in town. His Father told Clem to watch his bragging, because it may get him in trouble someday as somebody may call him on his boasting. Clem would shrug it off and say that he was the fastest gun in town. Elmer told his son that men may eventually come to prove that they were the fastest gun around, if word of Clem's supposed skill got out. He told Clem that he should spend more time on the horse farm than practicing how to kill men. Elmer said, "The farm will provide you with a future, but the gun fighting will take it away."

Eventually, it appeared that Elmer was right. The following week he faced his first challenge. He was approached by an old gunfighter named Lucas Black. He approached Clem and said, "I hear tell that you are the fastest gun in these parts, and I plan on putting you in the ground."

Clem knew that if he outdrew this gunfighter and killed him his reputation would start to grow, and he badly needed some recognition. He felt confident that he could beat Lucas Black. So confident that he told Lucas to pick out a nice tombstone for himself because he was going to need it.

Clem figured that for his first gunfight he should look the part; he went to the general store and purchased leather duds in black and a black holster as well. After that he felt ready. He told the old gunfighter to meet him at sunrise and also told him where he would be standing waiting for him. Clem knew that the sun at his back was a distinct advantage; the glare from it would sometimes temporarily blind an opponent. All those tiring hours of practicing were about to pay off; he was starting to feel good about himself.

The old gunfighter was there as scheduled.

Clem was glad there was no wind; he didn't need anything to alter his bullet's path. As the old man grabbed for his colt, Clem's hand moved at lightning speed. He was about to deliver a volley of shots at Lucas and watch him fall to the ground. In that split moment he recalled all the times when he was practicing imagining the look on his opponents face.

Clem's gun was drawn long before the old man's. While he was standing there the crowd stood by in amazement. They couldn't believe their eyes. Clem was frozen in bewilderment. He couldn't bring himself to kill another human being, a feeling he hadn't counted on. He felt a burning sensation in his chest and realized that moment of hesitation was his undoing. As the bullet found its mark, Clem managed to get one shot off. It too found its mark in Lucas Black's head. He was killed instantly. As Clem was falling to the ground he thought about his dreams of becoming a legendary gunfighter. As Clem's body landed on that lonely street his life and his dreams had gone with him.

ABOUT THE AUTHOR

After writing three books of poetry I finally admitted to myself that most people don't read poetry let alone the four-line end rhyme style that I write. I decided to write a book of short stories. There are many stories in my new book, assorted stories for any ear. I'm a fan of Alfred Hitchcock, so I try to put a twist in every story that I write.

I realize that the years are moving on so I thought I'd take one more shot at writing. I quit drinking more than 25 years ago, and I have quit smoking over five years ago. I'm hoping to squeeze some additional years into my life span.

I really love to write. Besides spending time with my wife, there is nothing I would rather do with my time. (Oops, I forget bowling.) I have some unusual stories in this book including a lengthy one about my Basic Training experiences in the U.S. Army. This story is written so that anyone can understand the various escapades I encountered. It is quite humorous.

I have grown as a writer since I published my first book in 2005. The stories I have written for this book have more meaning and depth than the poetry I have previously written.

My time now will be spent promoting my two new books. I wrote a murder mystery that was to be included in my first book, but it was too long. It will be published by itself in my second publication. On occasion I also write made-to-order poetry for special occasions. This has proven to be an enjoyable side business for me. I've also written a few poems dedicated to my favorite city, Pittsburgh, PA. Some of those poems have found their way into my local newspaper.

I've spent my entire life in the city of Pittsburgh, Pa. There is no greater city in the world, and truthfully I feel sorry for people who don't live here. They don't know what they are missing. I believe that when I die I'll be leaving Pittsburgh, PA on earth and moving on to Pittsburgh, PA in heaven. My brother-in-law calls me the Pittsburgh Poet and, if that's true, it is an honor I carry with pride. Maybe I can add "The Short Story King" handle to that title.

So get yourself a cup of coffee or tea, no cigarettes or alcohol please, and snuggle up in your favorite chair and enter into some creations from my mind.

www.ingramcontent.com/pod-product-compliance
Lightning Source LLC
Chambersburg PA
CBHW060312260626
47160CB00007B/2583